The Tube Murder

By Hugh Morrison

MONTPELIER PUBLISHING
2025

© Hugh Morrison 2025

All rights reserved. No part of this publication may be reproduced, stored in a retrieval system, or transmitted, in any form or by any means without the prior written permission of the publisher, nor be otherwise circulated in any form of binding or cover other than that in which it is published and without a similar condition including this condition being imposed on the subsequent purchaser.

Published in Great Britain by Montpelier Publishing.
www.hughmorrisonbooks.com
Set in Palatino Linotype 10.5 point
Cover image by Miguna Studio
ISBN: 9798306219141

Follow Montpelier Publishing on Facebook

Chapter One

Evelyn Parks checked her reflection in the nearest window of the empty underground train carriage as it rattled and swayed its way through the north London suburbs. The glass, with dark night beyond, formed a blurred, makeshift mirror which she noted had roughly the same proportions as a cinema screen.

Glancing around quickly to assure herself that the carriage was empty, she practiced various expressions and poses, in a discreet and understated manner. The actresses in the new 'talkies', she remembered, had a different style to the old silent stars and she didn't want to appear old fashioned by overdoing it.

She giggled to herself, hardly believing her luck. Was she really going to be in a picture? It didn't seem possible. She knew she was pretty; she was slightly built with naturally blonde hair, large blue eyes and an upturned nose, and she instinctively turned this to her advantage, but nobody before had seriously suggested she might make it as an actress.

It was a shame there had been that silly argument at the station, almost a scene, but fortunately there didn't seem to be many people around to notice. She hated leaving him on bad terms like that. He would come round, she thought to herself. How could he not? Why would he want to stay with that drab wife of his?

Evelyn settled back into the upholstery of the train seat, wondering if there would be enough hot water left for a bath when she got home.

Home. She snorted mentally. Well, she would soon see the back of *that* place, with its weird elderly residents and that tight-fisted landlady. She was 'going places', as the saying went.

There was a blast of noise as the train entered a tunnel; suddenly the mirror effect was heightened now that only the absolute pitch black of the tunnel walls showed behind the mirror. Evelyn looked at herself and frowned. Did she have a double chin, or was it a trick of the light?

Too much of that heavy suet pudding her landlady served up, she thought to herself. She felt her mouth water a little. Despite the dangers of stodgy food, she did have something of a sweet tooth. No more chocolates though, she noted to herself. The film camera, so she had read in *Picturegoer*, made one look ten pounds heavier. Or was it ten stone? Surely not. She resolved, however, that she would have a 'gasper' every time she felt the urge from now on, as she remembered reading somewhere that they helped you lose weight.

She reached into her little handbag and produced a packet of ten Players. She looked up and noticed it was one of the two non-smoking carriages on the train, but decided to chance it; nobody was likely to see her.

Then she heard a 'clunk' and realised the door at the end of the carriage was open. Had it loosened itself? She had known that to happen sometimes. Or was it…There was a figure in the doorway, silhouetted against the light coming from the next carriage. She saw no peaked cap or uniform; it was not the guard coming to tick her off for smoking.

She briefly wondered, with a stab of visceral fear, who the person was. Then her eyes widened as she realised the figure had come close – much too close, and an instant later, she felt strong hands wrapped in cloth gripping her neck. Her last act in her short life was to attempt to cry out, but when she tried, no sound came, like the scream of someone in a nightmare.

Earlier that evening in a large, decaying Victorian house on the western edge of Hampstead, Clarice Thompson checked her reflection in the slightly stained, mahogany framed mirror of her dressing table as the dinner gong sounded downstairs.

At 21 her face had the bloom of youth but she was what men call 'pretty' rather than beautiful. Fair, with hair closer to brown than blonde cut in a fashionable crop. With judicious application of cosmetics, wearing her best frock and with her hair done a certain way, and her spectacles consigned to her handbag, she could turn men's heads; but she rarely chose to.

She had learned early on that making oneself attractive to men, as a species in general, did not enable one to choose *which* men were attracted to her, and the men who responded were invariably the ones whom she wanted nothing to do with.

Men like Mr Grocott for example, the principal of the secretarial college she attended. 'The Octopus' was his nickname amongst the girls (some of the less well-bred students had a worse name for him), and she soon found out why. After a close shave with him alone in his office, she noticed that he tended to confine his pestering to the more gaudily dressed girls, and thereafter she adopted a plainer, more businesslike appearance.

She liked it, anyway, she thought as she looked in the mirror. Spectacles suited her, she had been told several times, and the sober business suit she had had made at a bargain price by a little dressmaker in Camden Town lent her an air of gravitas she hoped would stand her in good stead when it came to looking for work.

Work! The word suggested, at times, a world of impossible glamour; of taking shorthand notes at the desk of some great industrialist whom she would then accompany on a business trip to New York on an ocean liner. She laughed grimly to herself and blinked the vision away. She was old and cynical enough to realise that in all probability her working life would consist of dodging the likes of Mr Grocott in some grim office overlooking a bypass road.

She stepped out of her little room onto the large, high ceilinged landing of the boarding house. She was about to knock for Evelyn next door, but remembered that she had gone out for the evening and so instead she walked down the stairs, taking care to avoid the loose stair-rod near the top.

She made her way into the dining room, with its ridiculously wide double doors, built to accommodate ladies in crinoline, and its equally ridiculous high ceiling, which immediately swallowed up the tiny amount of heat put out by the fireplace.

She seated herself at her usual table. The boarding house prided itself on separate tables, but in reality, the tables were so close together that the separation provided no privacy, and so the boast was meaningless. But that, thought Clarice, was The Hovel all over. She smiled at her own nickname for the place. Lovell Villa was the actual name of the establishment, or to give it its full title, the Lovell Villa Private Hotel, 87 Lovell Gardens, London,

NW3. The NW3 postal district was, like the separate tables, another piece of gentility that the landlady, Mrs Sibley, clung to fiercely.

The house lay perilously close to the border with NW6, and to Mrs Sibley that codification indicated a descent into such horrors as windows without nets, Irish immigrants, and barrel-organs in the street. Before the war, when this particular quadrant of the capital had all just been London NW, such social stratifications had been far less distinct.

Clarice received the usual nods, smiles and 'good evenings' from the other residents, and as she removed the slightly soiled napkin from its ring and placed it on her lap, she looked around at them.

There was little Miss Grant, an elderly spinster who sat alone at the rickety table by the door, and who never seemed to eat anything; Clarice suspected she was hard up as she spent her evenings in the lounge darning and mending and rarely went out.

Between her and Clarice sat the Stewarts. Alec Stewart was large, jovial, spoke with an Edinburgh accent, and was Something in Tea. He made much of the fact that he and his wife had spent several years in Darjeeling and then Bombay.

They cannot, thought Clarice, have ever amounted to much, or they would not now be living in virtual penury, but to hear Mr Stewart talk you would think he had been little less than Governor General of India, and of course Mrs Sibley lapped that up.

Added to this social cachet was the fact that Mr Stewart drove a little motor-car to work, paid for by his firm, which he kept in the gimcrack mock-tudor asbestos garage by the side of the house; Mrs Sibley was forever attempting to cadge lifts in order to be seen out motoring by her friends, but Mr Stewart usually managed to forestall this with a jaunty 'business use only, I'm afraid, Mrs S!'

His wife Mary, who was dark, with the hint of a Welsh accent and the suggestion of once having been quite attractive, had a long suffering air and sometimes gave Clarice and Evelyn a weak smile if they were going out, and accompanied it with a hearty 'enjoy the bachelor life while you can, dears!'

Then there was Mr Hargrove, sitting by the window which looked out onto the sooty, darkened laurel bushes in the back garden. Middle-aged, but with a muscular, outdoors appearance, he seemed to live permanently under a cloud of self-absorption; he rarely spoke and nobody knew what he did or where he went. He had a military air about him, but never mentioned any service experience.

Then there was the New Man, Clifford Thorley, who called himself Cliff. He had not arrived in the dining room yet, but his place was kept next to Hargrove at the window, and the pair occasionally passed the time of day together. 'Not safe in taxis,' Evelyn had said of him using the sort of ridiculous expression she picked up from the American comedies in the cinema, but Clarice had failed to provide any evidence for this.

He was young – about 23 or so, and tall, but that was about all he had going in his favour. He didn't display any 'octopus' tendencies, but there was something not altogether trustworthy about him.

He was some sort of writer, though of what, nobody seemed quite sure. He typed away at all hours in his little attic room, smoked a filthy pipe and wore a suit of tweed of such thickness it could easily have doubled as carpet. His shoes looked as if they were made from the same leather as those squashed medieval relics one sees in museums, his hair was too long and he wore neither hat nor overcoat even in cold weather.

'Mr Thorley is late again, I see,' said Mrs Sibley as she entered the dining room. The remark was addressed to nobody in particular by the landlady, a stern, stout woman of indeterminate age with iron-grey hair who stood like a sentinel at the dining room door during mealtimes, as if daring anybody to leave without her permission.

'Well, we can't wait,' she continued. 'Serve the soup please, Vera.'

At this request the maid-of-all-work bustled into the room, whispering 'sorry' to nobody in particular, and began passing out the tepid soup bowls, one of which always seemed to be cracked. Fortunately, noticed Clarice, the cracked one did not seem to have gone to her this evening. She wondered if Mrs Sibley rotated them between the residents in the hope that it would not be noticed.

Poor Vera, thought Clarice, stooped and blinking behind her thick spectacles with her lace cap on askew. She was part of the dying breed of English domestic servant. If she had been pretty she would have got work on the cosmetics counter at Woolworth's; if she had been clever, she would have been employed in an office or as a skilled worker in one of the gleaming new factories on the North Circular Road. But she was neither pretty nor clever, and seemed destined for a life of domestic drudgery.

Clarice had initially wondered if Vera might be Mrs Sibley's natural daughter from some long ago liaison, or else why bother to employ such a hopeless case, but then she decided this was a flight of fantasy too far. Vera was probably just the best servant that the owner of the Lovell Villa Private Hotel could afford.

'Talk of the devil,' murmured Mr Stewart as he slurped his soup.

'Been at the Labour Exchange again, Thorley?' he said jovially as Cliff Thorley walked into the dining room.

'Hah!' The sharp, humourless ejaculation was Cliff's only reply to Mr Stewart's attempt at a joke. Clarice watched him as he sauntered across the room, ignoring the other diners, and plonked himself down at the table next to Hargrove by the window, to whom he gave the curtest of nods.

Clarice caught a whiff of something sulphurous and noticed that Cliff had his pipe in his hand. Pipe smoke, as far as she could tell, came in two varieties: the kind that smelled pleasantly sweet, like something wafting from a bakery, or the kind that smelled like india-rubber tyres smouldering on a bonfire. Cliff's type was the latter.

'No smoking in the dining room, if you please, Mr Thorley,' snapped Mrs Sibley.

'Ah,' shrugged Cliff. He got up slowly and placed the pipe between his teeth. He puffed experimentally but no smoke came.

'Never mind, gone out anyway,' he said. Then to the astonishment of the other diners he walked to the fireplace, tapped the pipe twice on the chimney-piece, and brushed the resulting heap of ashes into the tiny pile of smouldering coal in the grate.

'A little more fuel for the fire,' he said to nobody in particular, and sat back down to begin clattering around with his soup spoon.

Clarice could not help smiling; she suppressed the grin when she saw the expression on Mrs Sibley's face, which was one of confused horror.

'I am sure Mr Thorley meant nothing by it,' piped up Miss Grant. 'As a newcomer, he has yet to adjust to our ways, wouldn't you agree, Mrs Sibley?'

'Quite so, Miss Grant,' said Mrs Sibley. 'We do have

rather a high proportion of new residents.'

This, Clarice had noticed over the course of her two weeks' tenancy, was one of the perennial themes of conversation in the hotel. She guessed what was coming next.

'I, of course, am the last of the Old Guard,' said Miss Grant, with a proud smile. 'I shall have lived here 32 years come next Whitsun.'

'Long service medal coming up then, eh?' joked Mr Stewart. Clarice noticed he occasionally proffered military remarks in the direction of Mr Hargrove, perhaps in an attempt to draw him out, but it never worked. Nobody laughed; the rattle of spoons on soup plates continued, blending with the sound of politely restrained slurping.

Clarice shuddered inwardly. 32 years, that meant Miss Grant had been in this same house since 1899. She did not dislike the old lady, but found it hard to imagine what sort of a life one could have for that long in such a place as this, like some living ghost haunting a well-trodden route up and down the stairs each day.

God forbid, she prayed earnestly, I end up like her.

The brief but fervent devotion was interrupted by Vera clattering the plates for the main course; lukewarm mutton with stewed cabbage and potatoes. Mrs Sibley did not allow sauce bottles on the tables – presumably, thought Clarice, she considered them in some way 'common', or perhaps she just did not like the expense. At any rate, there was nothing to make the food palatable and so she began chewing rapidly and regularly in order to get the whole affair over with as quickly as possible.

'People do seem to move around an awful lot these days,' said Mrs Stewart. 'Mr Stewart and myself have only been here six months, although we didn't come far. Our previous property was not up to our standards so it was a blessed relief to leave. Mr Hargrove joined us, I think, three months ago; and the new young people have each only been here less than a month, I believe.'

'You must have been one of the first lot in, Miss Grant,' said Mr Stewart in-between mouthfuls. 'When was the place set up?'

He looked at Mrs Sibley but no answer was forthcoming; Clarice had noticed she did not like to make polite conversation during meals, presumably seeing herself as the equivalent of a schoolmistress charged with looking after slightly backward children.

'Mrs Sibley inherited the house shortly before I moved here,' said Miss Grant proudly, as if the bequest was somehow of her own doing. 'She and the late Mr Sibley opened it as a private hotel. Prior to that it was a family house, owned, I believe, by the chairman of a prominent bank. Am I correct, Mrs Sibley?'

Mrs Sibley merely nodded, and began taking away the plates of those who had finished. She rarely divulged anything of her past and always seemed slightly affronted when Miss Grant brought the subject up. The 'late Mr Sibley' in particular seemed to be a taboo subject. Clarice wondered whether he was really dead, or if he had actually deserted her and the 'late' prefix was a polite euphemism.

'Yes indeed,' continued Miss Grant wistfully, seemingly unconscious of the fact that Mrs Sibley had not replied. 'It was considered rather "fast" for an unmarried girl to live in a private hotel in those days. I was something of a "New Woman", I suppose.'

Clarice smiled. It was hard to imagine Miss Grant ever having been 'fast' in any sense of the word. She finished the last of the lukewarm food on her plate just as Vera clumsily scooped it away and placed a bowl containing a yellow substance in front of her.

'Ah, pudding!' exclaimed Mr Stewart. He had said that every evening since she had moved here, thought Clarice, as if it were some novel event rather than something completely predictable.

Clarice poked disconsolately at the bowl. Prunes and custard again; one of two or three puddings that were rotated, none of which were particularly appetising. She heard the sharp scrape of a chair in the corner and looked up to see Cliff striding out of the room, his pudding left untouched. Mrs Sibley, still standing guard at the door, looked at him as if he had just sworn in church.

'Off his food,' observed Mrs Stewart with something of a maternal air.

'Wants to leave more room for beer, I expect,' said her husband conspiratorially. 'More fool him, when there's good food like this,' he added, returning to his pudding.

After dinner the routine at the Lovell Hotel was invariably the same; the residents gathered in the sitting room, or the 'drawing room' as Mrs Sibley insisted on calling it, for coffee. The word coffee was used in its loosest possible sense; the brown liquid served was Paterson's Camp Coffee heavily diluted with a large quantity of milk and sugar whether one wanted it or not.

After this the residents would take part in various semi-private activities such as reading, crossword puzzles, knitting and the like until ten p.m. An official 'lights out' did not form part of the rules but it was an unspoken agreement between tenants and landlady that no intercourse of any kind would take place after that time.

Clarice intended to have only a quick cup of coffee and then retire to the privacy of her room to study her Pitman shorthand book. When she entered the sitting room she found herself alone with Cliff, the others not having finished their puddings.

He had lit his pipe again and Clarice recoiled slightly at the acrid smell. Smoking was not expressly forbidden in the sitting room, but the other residents rarely indulged, and never in the sitting room. Mrs Sibley left the residents to their own devices after supper, and so the topic was rarely mentioned, although sometimes Mrs Stewart would make a pointed remark such as 'what unusual tobacco, Mr Thorley,' which was met by an non-committal grunt in return.

Cliff must have read Clarice's mind, because he tapped the pipe out again, this time in an ashtray rather than the grate; the sitting room had the luxury of a gas fire.

'Needs a clean,' he said. 'We haven't had much of a chance to chat, have we?'

'No, we haven't,' said Clarice non-committally as she took a cup of coffee from the sideboard, choosing the one with the least amount of chips in it. He really was a most peculiar looking fellow, she decided.

That suit! Complemented by the sort of itchy-looking shirt that soldiers wore, with an attached collar, always unbuttoned, and a tie that appeared to have been hand knitted, like some sort of narrow scarf. He had no waistcoat, and instead wore a pullover with several holes in it, made either by moths or pipe cinders, or perhaps both.

'Your girlfriend not joining the merry band this evening?' he asked.

'If you mean Miss Parks,' said Clarice, 'she's gone out.'

'And left poor Cinderella alone?'

The cheek of him! Clarice bridled at the remark and felt herself blushing. She resolved to stand her ground with this man and not betray the least emotion.

'I assumed you two were bosom pals,' he continued.

'Not really,' said Clarice. 'We attend the same secretarial college. It was she who recommended this place.'

'Ah. Your people not from London then?'

'No.'

'Up country somewhere, I assume?'

'If you must know, my parents are dead. Until I turned twenty-one I lived with an aunt in Bedfordshire.'

'Well, well. Our family seat, what's left of it, is in Northants, so we're near neighbours.'

Clarice's curiosity was aroused now and she felt herself strangely drawn into the conversation with this peculiar individual.

'And what brings you to the Hovel?' she asked jocularly.

'The what?'

'The Hovel. That's what Miss Parks and I call this place.'

'Hah!' exclaimed Cliff. 'I say, that's awfully good. Hovel-Lovell. A near rhyme, or is it a para-rhyme?'

Clarice felt herself blushing again and resolved to be serious. 'You're some sort of writer, I take it?'

'Trying to be,' said Cliff. 'Independent journalist. What they call a 'freelancer.' I was on a paper in Northampton after coming down from the varsity, but one rather tires of reporting church fetes and dog shows after a while. Thought I'd have a go at starving in a garret in Hampstead.'

'You're hardly likely to starve with what Mrs Sibley serves up.'

'Only if one eats it. I may not be starving but at least I *am* in a garret. I hate to sound like a snob but I only put up with this place because it's cheap and has a Hampstead address. It goes down better with editors, you see. A mile either way and my letters would be post-marked Kilburn or Golders Green and professionally that would be the end of me. Hampstead fulfills the stereotype of the romantic writer. They assume I must be living in some sort of Georgian idyll, inspired by the ghosts of Keats and Browning. I say, Browning *has* died, hasn't he?'

Clarice laughed instinctively. 'Years ago!' she exclaimed.

'Poetry's not my thing really,' said Cliff. 'You?'

'Not particularly.'

'Good girl. Like walking?'

'I love the Heath. It's one of the best things about this place, being so near.'

'Grand, isn't it?' I say, we must go for a stroll there one day.'

This was said with such an honest expression that Clarice felt absolutely no sensation of being 'picked up', as Evelyn would have put it. Was he even interested in girls, she wondered. One heard rumours about writers, but there didn't seem to be anything the slightest bit effeminate about him.

Before Clarice had a chance to reply, there was a sound of voices from the hallway outside.

'Must go,' said Cliff, draining the last of the coffee from his cup. 'The spirits are gathering. Well, cheerio.'

Clarice watched as he squeezed past Miss Grant on her way into the lounge.

'Off out again, I see,' said the elderly lady. 'All the men in this establishment seem to disappear as quickly as possible after dinner. A pity; there are never enough of us to make up a good rubber. Remind me, do you play bridge, dear?'

'Sorry, I never learned,' replied Clarice.

'Perhaps I shall teach you.'

'That's very kind of you Miss Grant, but I must press on. I have a shorthand test tomorrow and ought to revise.'

'Ah yes, of course,' said Miss Grant wistfully, as she looked doubtfully at the coffee cups on the sideboard.

'Mind you don't strain your eyes. Mrs Sibley does insist on giving us those rather dim light bulbs.'

Clarice smiled and said nothing, then made her way upstairs to her room. She was just in time to see Cliff slipping out of the front door into the misty darkness.

Two hours later Clarice put down her book on shorthand and rubbed her eyes; Miss Grant was right about the poor light in the bedrooms, and she made a mental note to buy a brighter bulb; nobody need know since the lamp was never on when Vera did out the rooms.

Lying in bed (the rooms were always unheated, so she got under the covers as soon as she could), she looked around. It wasn't a bad room, she thought; it had been the last she had seen after an exhausting search the day she had come to London.

Londoners, she had come to realise, were forced to partake in a titanic struggle to secure a tiny piece of space for themselves, like shipwrecked seafarers jostling for a place on a raft. If one could find something remotely habitable, one clung to it for dear life.

The 'Hovel' was cheap, at least by London standards. She would rather have lived in some bright ladies' hostel with social functions and a wireless in the lounge, but such places charged high rents and there was always a waiting list. A small bed-sitting room would have suited her better, as she enjoyed cooking and was able to fend for herself economically, but again, such places as she had seen were far too expensive for the small private income she had inherited on her mother's death.

There was also a sort of grim gentility at the Lovell Villa

Private Hotel which made it just about bearable. For a young single girl in London it was the bottom rung on the ladder of respectability. Below that yawned the chasm of lodgings with families in far-flung suburbs at the ends of tram routes, in houses with worn linoleum and noisy children, smelling of boiled cabbage and dustbins.

She had seen one or two of those places and that was enough for her. Or, she could have shared a bedsitting room with another girl, but that thought repelled her as well. To be cooped up with a stranger in a single room in a London winter! Privacy was important to her and she was willing to pay a little extra for it.

She wound the little travel alarm clock by her bed and looked at the dial. Nearly eleven o'clock. She had heard once or twice the front door open and the sound of cautious male footsteps on the stairs.

She realised Miss Grant was right; the male residents did seem to go out a lot. Presumably, she thought, to pubs, or perhaps even clubs. Mr Stewart occasionally mentioned 'his club' but never by name. He did the same when referring to his school; it was always anonymous, which suggested it was probably below par.

One could hardly blame the men for wanting to go out at night, she supposed; listening to Miss Grant's interminable church gossip, or Mrs Stewart commenting on the plots of her romantic novels from Boots' library, was enough to drive anyone to drink.

Evelyn had still not come home. Mrs Sibley locked the front door at eleven; this was one of the rules of the house which were typed on a yellowing sheet of foolscap and pasted to the inside of the door of each room. Evelyn had been coy about where she was going and Clarice couldn't help thinking that meant she was out with a man.

She turned off the lamp and pulled the covers over her.

She then felt a twinge of fear as she remembered Evelyn saying something rather worrying to her a few days ago. Evelyn had dismissed her concerns with a sort of big-sisterly jollity. It was probably nothing, she had said.

Then she experienced a sudden sense of panic. What if her friend had had an accident in the fog, and was lying somewhere in the dark, unseen, as people and vehicles passed within a few feet of her?

She shuddered, and told herself not to be so stupid. She was probably at some dance-hall and had forgotten the time. She smiled to think of what extraordinary scenes would take place when she returned home to find the front door locked and had to rouse Mrs Sibley. At least it would bring a little life into the place!

Chapter Two

The large black motor car ground its way up the long, tree-lined incline leading from central London to the suburb of Hampstead. A uniformed constable in a peaked cap was at the wheel, and two men sat on the back seat.

Detective Inspector George Travers looked out at the fog-wreathed autumnal night with its shimmering gas-lamps which struggled to relieve the gloom. He was a man in early middle age, of average height and build but somehow giving the impression of greater stature.

He was one of the new breed of sleek, professional and classless men which had emerged since the war; able to operate competently in any setting, from the drawing rooms of Belgravia to the slums of Whitechapel, but never fully at home in any of them.

He rubbed his eyes; he had been woken by the insistent ringing of the telephone bell summoning him to Hampstead, and moments later had been picked up by his driver.

'What do we know so far?' He turned to his companion, Detective Sergeant Bill Hollis, who had his eyes closed.

'Wake up,' urged Travers, politely but firmly. 'You're on nights, I'm not and I'm wide awake.'

'Sorry sir,' said Hollis. He was younger than Travers but had the world-weary air of the harassed paterfamilias. His superior, by contrast, had neither wife nor children, and was not greatly disturbed by being called out at any time of the day or night.

'Young girl found strangled on an underground train. Morden-Edgware line,' said Hollis. 'Local chaps telephoned Scotland Yard as their only CID men are off on another job.'

'Hang on,' said Travers. 'Underground train, you say? They've got their own police.'

'Yes, but they've already handed over to us. Not set up for this sort of thing. Pickpockets is about their limit.'

Travers was glad his assistant understood the administrative complexities of the various enforcers of the law in London; he found it a tedious subject which sometimes prevented him from the efficient execution of his duties.

'Thought so,' replied the Inspector. 'Good to make sure though. We don't want to tread on any toes we don't have to. How old was the girl?'

'About twenty, sir. I only took the barest details on the telephone. We're here now, I think.'

The north London streets were empty and desolate at this late hour, and one of the few electric lights visible shone from the ticket office of Hampstead underground station.

'Park up here, Barnes,' said Travers to the driver, who edged the car into a small gap between the road and the station. Travers noted another light, from an all-night tea stall across the road frequented by taxi drivers. 'Get yourself a cup of tea, but don't go too far, eh?'

'Sir,' replied the driver with a grin. Travers was known for remembering names and going easy on men who had to wait on him for long periods of time, a quality that endeared him to them just as it had endeared the men in his company in France during the war.

A constable met them at the ticket barrier and escorted them in the rattling lift down to station level. As the attendant opened the lift gates, there was a blast of warm air and the smell of something institutional that might have been disinfectant blended with brake dust.

After a walk along curved, tiled corridors they emerged onto the dimly-lit platform, deserted except for a small crowd of men at one end standing around a form on the platform covered with a tarpaulin.

Travers introduced himself and soon distinguished the relevant persons from the official hangers-on. A nervous looking man in railway uniform presented himself.

'Fred Watkins, station master,' said the man. 'I'm the one who found her.' He indicated the tarpaulin-covered body at his feet. At that moment there was a roar of sound and a train rushed into the station; a hiss of pneumatic doors and a handful of late travellers looked curiously towards the end of the platform as they alighted.

'Can't you get this place shut down?' asked Travers.

'That's the last southbound train,' said Watkins. 'It'll be quiet from now on.'

'Good. Let's have a look at her then.'

Travers gently lifted the tarpaulin and looked at the dead girl. She looked peaceful, almost as if she were sleeping; the only indication she had died a violent death were the blackening weals around her pale throat.

'Which one's the doctor?' asked Travers.

An elderly medical man was summoned before the Inspector and gave his account.

'I live nearby and came as soon as our local constable knocked on my door,' he said querulously. 'There was nothing I could do. She must have been dead when she was found. May I go now, you see, I have a patient to attend to in the…'

'One moment please,' said Travers. 'Cause of death?'

'I really couldn't say…' hesitated the doctor.

'Hazard a guess, sir?' pressed the Inspector.

'Asphyxiation, given the marks.'

'Has she been…that is, is there any sign of…'

'You can hardly expect me to check for *that* on a public railway platform,' interrupted the doctor. 'A post-mortem will tell you.'

'Very well. How long's she been dead?'

'Rigor mortis has not set in…in fact the body was almost warm when I examined her. I should say she died very recently, perhaps momentarily, before she was found. Now I really must…'

'Yes, yes, thank you doctor,' said Travers, dismissing the man. 'We'll get the Yard doctor down here as soon as we can.'

With an air of relief the doctor strode away towards the lifts. Travers turned to Watkins.

'Died before she was found,' said the Inspector. 'Why on earth did you take her off the train?'

'I wasn't sure she *was* dead when I found her,' insisted the station master. 'I just assumed she'd been taken ill. See, I was on my rounds down here when the train pulled in. The party in question, that is, the deceased dead party, was on her own in one of the middle carriages. Stopped just by me. I barely noticed her, thought she was asleep, but then she slumped forward and fell right down on the floor.'

'What happened then?' interjected Travers.

'Well, I thought to myself, hello, someone's had a drop too much. We get that sometimes, but not usually with a respectable-looking young girl like that. So I shouted for the guard to hold the doors, and had a look. White as a sheet she was, all folded over forwards like, with her head on the seat opposite. I didn't like the look of her one bit. So

I called for the guard and we took her off. That was when we realised she was dead.'

'Where's the guard?' asked Travers.

'He had to go, we couldn't hold the train up. We kept it here ten minutes as it was.'

'I don't suppose you saw anyone in the carriage?'

'She was on her own, like I said. Nobody in the carriage on either side as far as I recall, though there were a couple in the front carriage I think. Didn't see anyone much on the train at all. They're usually near empty at this time on a week night going south. Besides, I barely had time to look.'

Travers sighed. 'And you let the whole bally train roll on? There could have been evidence in there.'

'Now look here, governor,' protested the station master. 'You've got your job to do, we've got ours. We can't just hold a train indefinitely, the whole system would back up and we'd have people stuck in tunnels from here to the other side of London. It's like telling someone's blood to stop circulating.'

The official crossed his arms and looked defiantly at Travers.

'All right, Mr Watkins, you did your best,' said Travers affably. 'I'd've liked to have seen that carriage though.'

'You still can,' said the station master proudly. 'I'm not stupid you know. I got the guard to isolate the doors on that carriage so's they wouldn't open. We can do that, you see. Took the serial number as well. She went through to Morden but will most likely be back at the northern depot by now. If you get there quick you'll see it before they let the fluffers on.'

'Fluffers?'

'The chars. They do out all the carriages every night.'

'We can't have *that*,' said Travers. 'Where's the depot?'

'Golders Green, next stop up the line. The guard works

out of there so they can give you his details there too.'

'This depot on the telephone?'

'Of course. I can get through from my office.'

'Well run and tell them – now if you please – to keep the, er, fluffers off that carriage until we get there.'

'Well, I…that is, we're closing up now'.

'I'm not asking, I'm telling. There could be vital evidence in there and I'm not having some Mrs Mop ruining it. You don't want a charge of obstruction, do you?'

At this, Watkins ceased his objections and hurried away to his office. A police constable then appeared from the platform exit, leading two solemn looking ambulance-men who were carrying a canvas stretcher.

Travers took a last look at the girl and replaced the tarpaulin, then nodded at the ambulance-men.

'I'll take that,' he said, as the girl's hand-bag was moved aside during the process of placing her body on the stretcher. 'At least that shows us the motive was unlikely to be robbery.'

He dismissed the rest of the hangers-on. Lights were dimmed as the station closed; a service train rumbled through at half-speed, and then all was quiet.

'Not much to go on,' remarked Hollis.

'There's always something,' replied Travers as he rummaged through the dead girl's reticule. There was something pathetic, he thought, in its small size and gaudy design, inlaid with imitation pearls.

'Like this for example,' he continued, opening a letter. 'My dear Evie etc etc, your loving mother etc etc. Addressed to Miss Parks, the Lovell Villa Private Hotel, 87 Lovell Gardens London NW3. That gives us her name and address. And a next of kin, mother, a Mrs Parks, presumably, of…of…why can't people write properly…18 Cadogan, or Cardigan something, Southend-on-Sea, Essex.

Look it up. And what's this?'

He fumbled in the bag and picked out a small piece of printed cardboard.

'Underground ticket,' he said. 'Today's date. Single, for threepence, bought at Brent. Where's that?'

'Two stops up this line,' said Hollis, glancing at the painted metal route sign on the wall opposite.

'Can't remember the last time I took the tube,' said Travers. 'How do these things work nowadays?'

'Well sir, that ticket means she got on at Brent. We can't say where she was going, as a threepenny fare takes you pretty much anywhere and the tickets don't specify the destination.'

'Let's not worry too much about where she might have been going,' said Travers. 'Let's concentrate on where she's been. Brent, then what's the next stop, Golders Green, then here. She was found here at, what time?'

'23.03 precisely, sir,' said Hollis, after consulting his notes. 'All the trains keep to a tight schedule.'

'How long would it have taken her to get from Brent?'

'About ten to 15 minutes, I'd say. I normally reckon on journeys taking about five minutes between stations on the tube, but it varies.'

'I'll take your word for it. So she would have got on at Brent some time after 10.45pm. Right then, get over to…no, it's too late now, they'll be off home. First thing tomorrow I want men interviewing anyone and everyone working or travelling on the line between Brent and Hampstead this evening, anyone who might have seen something. And put out a call in the papers for anyone with information. We'll get the usual cranks but it might turn up something.'

Hollis scribbled furiously on his notepad, then looked up. 'What about the carriage, sir?'

'Blast, I was forgetting,' said Travers. 'Lack of sleep.'

Hollis raised his eyebrows but said nothing.

'We'll get round there straight away,' continued Travers. 'While I'm having a look you telephone through to the Yard and get the ball rolling. Tell the brass we need every available man. And I want a round-up – I want every sex-pest, every ticket-of-leave man with a record of violence against women in the whole of London brought in. If we're lucky it will be someone we already know.'

'What about the next of kin, sir?' asked Hollis wearily.

'Get the Southend police to…no, on second thoughts get yourself down there first thing on the train. It's only, what, three quarters of an hour from Fenchurch Street. Break it to them before the papers get hold of it, it's too late for the morning but it will be in the evening ones and it might even be on the lunchtime wireless bulletin. Find out all you can, you know, workplace, private life, boy-friends and so on, and we'll reconvene in the afternoon.'

'There's the girl's lodgings as well, sir,' said Hollis.

'I'll have a look round tomorrow – that is, today,' replied Travers. 'Now, let's get to this depot place before anyone tramples on something vital. With any luck he's left his name in blood on the window or something.'

Hollis smiled grimly. 'Stranglers don't tend to leave bloodstains, sir.'

'You take things too seriously,' said Travers.

The lights flickered, and then went out; the platform was lit only by an eerie purple light which came from some sort of emergency system.

'What the devil…?' exclaimed Travers. Suddenly he felt a chilling sensation; the dim platform with its yawning black tunnel ahead looked distinctly unnerving.

A lamp flashed at the other end of the platform.

'Hi there,' shouted Travers. 'Put those ruddy lights back on.'

'We're closing. I thought you'd gone.' It was Watkins, the station master, who waved a flickering paraffin lamp.

'Well we haven't,' said Travers. 'And I don't want to fall head-first onto a live rail so if you would be so kind, perhaps you might show us to the lifts.'

Watkins chuckled. 'Current's off now for when the fluffers come. You'd probably just sprain an ankle. This way, gents.'

The two detectives followed the station master out, leaving behind the blackened tunnels, as dark and silent as a tomb.

A mile or so away, the Lovell Villa Private Hotel lay almost equally dark and silent. Almost, because a single, low-wattage electric bulb served to illuminate both the hallway and the first-floor landing. Although Mrs Sibley disliked the expense of such a facility, she had formed the idea that it was somehow a deterrent against burglars, and that therefore, as she would say, 'all things considered' it was worthwhile expenditure.

The front door of the hotel was locked and bolted each night precisely at 11pm. Mrs Sibley paid no heed to whether her boarders were at home or not by that hour; if they were not (and she could not remember such an occurrence) they were expected to find alternative accommodation until the door was re-opened at 6.30 in the morning.

This rule was foremost in the mind of one of the residents, who walked silently up the black and white tiled garden path (he was wearing rubber-soled shoes). At the front door he gently tried his latch-key, but only for a moment, as he was not expecting it to work.

After a brief glance at the street behind him, he stepped over the dusty laurel bushes by the large bay window of the lounge. He extracted a certain article from his coat pocket and with it performed a certain manouevre, familiar to the criminal classes, upon the catch of the sash window. After raising it gently, he deftly climbed through and closed it behind him, and made his way up to bed.

How many kinds of sweet flowers grow
In an English country garden?
We'll tell you now of some that we know
Those we miss you'll surely pardon
Daffodils, heart's ease and flox
Meadowsweet and lady smocks
Gentian, lupine and tall hollihocks...

The scratched gramophone record poured out the tinkling sound of the bucolic song into the distinctly un-floral surroundings of the Camden Town Secretarial College. A row of young women sat at battered desks, each one equipped with an ancient black typewriter. The trainee typists clattered along with the jaunty rhythm of the music, as they typed out the lyrics of the song. After each second line there was a resounding 'ting' as all the carriages were returned at the same time.

All except one. Clarice had somehow got her finger stuck between the keys, and was only able to return the carriage two seconds later than everyone else. Miss French, the tutor, frowned and crossed the room to see what was going on.

Clarice looked down and her heart sank; the last line she had typed was 'dafolids, hearts' tease and fox' and it was now too late to pick up the rhythm again. She fumbled with the carriage return and tried to find her place on the keys.

She was expecting a ticking off from Miss French, but it did not come. The tutor was summoned to the door by Mr Grocott, who pointed at Clarice. Miss French beckoned her over.

'Would you come this way?' asked Mr Grocott. His eyes quickly appraised her from head to toe, a habit he had with every one of the college's pupils.

Clarice was shown into Mr Grocott's office. A man she had never seen before was seated at the desk. He rose politely to his feet.

'Miss Thompson? Won't you sit down?'

He indicated another chair and Clarice sat, while Mr Grocott and Miss French watched suspiciously from a corner of the room. The man was not exactly handsome, she thought, but had a pleasant, avuncular face and he was well dressed, with a coloured tie that echoed the blue stripe in the cloth of his suit.

'My name is Detective Inspector Travers,' said the man. 'From Scotland Yard. Am I right in saying that you share lodgings with a Miss Evelyn Parks?'

Clarice's stomach lurched. It was nearly lunchtime, and she always felt as if she had a slightly upset stomach when she was hungry, but this time a stab of fear made the sensation worse. So something *had* happened to Evelyn. When she did not appear at breakfast, she had tried to pretend to herself she had stayed out all night somewhere; perhaps even somewhere not entirely disreputable, such as an all-night cafe; she had missed the last tube, and then…but it was no good. The policeman was speaking to her again.

'I said are you all right, Miss Thompson?'

'Quite well, thank you. Miss Parks and I live in the same boarding house, yes. I assume there has been an accident.'

Clarice always thought it was best to grasp the nettle in these cases, and get the worst over with.

'Not exactly,' continued Travers. 'Something more serious. Miss Parks was found dead yesterday night, on an underground train at Hampstead.'

Clarice felt her vision become liquid, as if she were at the bottom of a swimming bath. She blinked, and breathed deeply. 'How did it happen?' she asked.

'I am sorry to say we believe she was murdered. Death was caused by strangulation. It appears to have been mercifully quick.'

This was the worst, the very worst, thought Clarice to herself; it could not get worse now. She must be strong.

'You look pale,' said Travers with concern. 'I say there, Miss, ah, French. Could you make us some tea?'

Miss French looked somewhat taken aback, as if tea-making were beneath her duties, even in such a crisis as this, but Mr Grocott nodded and she briskly left the room in the direction of the tea urn in the corridor.

'Perhaps you would lend a hand, sir?' said Travers, in the manner of one who does not expect to receive a reply in the negative.

Grocott mumbled 'of course,' and followed the tutor out of the room.

Travers took out a gold case from his pocket and opened it in front of Clarice.

'Cigarette?'

'No thank you.'

'Very well. Don't mind if I smoke?'

'Of course not.'

Travers lit his cigarette and exhaled a long plume of smoke upwards.

'Thank you for taking this so calmly, Miss Thompson,' he said. 'It does make a difficult job rather easier. Unfortunately I am well used to this sort of conversation but I realise you are not. I'd like to ask a few questions but please take your time in answering.'

Clarice nodded. 'Have you…'

'I'd appreciate it if you let me ask the questions first, Miss Thompson,' said the Inspector firmly, but not unkindly. 'Then you can ask me anything you like. How does that sound?'

'Very well.'

'Good. Now, I expect your first thought is, have we caught the person who did it? The answer to that is no, but I hope to make an arrest very soon and we're following a number of lines of enquiry. Miss Parks's mother has already been informed and she told one of my men that Evelyn was training at this establishment. Mr Grocott then told me that you and her were friends, is that right? Ah, talk of the devil.'

Mr Grocott looked puzzled at this attempt at a jocular remark as he and Miss French placed tea cups in front of the Inspector and Clarice. The two pedagogues hovered uncertainly around the desk.

'Perhaps you would go and supervise the other, ah, young ladies with their studies,' said Travers. 'You can tell them we may need to speak to them but for now I'd like to interview Miss Thompson alone.'

Mr Grocott and Miss French took the hint and left the room. Within a few moments the sound of the gramophone and the clattering typewriters resumed outside the private office.

'I'm glad I caught you here,' said Travers, 'as the

evening editions of the newspapers will be out soon and it would be an awful shock to read about your friend in them without being forewarned. These journalists seem to have a sixth sense about these things happening.' He sipped his tea, looking at Clarice over the cup as he did so.

'As I said,' he continued, 'we're following a number of lines of enquiry but in these cases it's often the nearest and dearest that can tell us the most.'

'I'd hardly call her nearest and dearest,' protested Clarice glumly. 'I'd barely known her a month.'

'I see,' said Travers. 'Did she have many friends in London? Boy-friends, and so on?'

'I don't think so. And she didn't have a particular boy-friend,' said Clarice.

The Inspector almost imperceptibly raised an official eyebrow.

'I don't mean she knew lots of men,' said Clarice quickly. 'I mean she went dancing, and to the cinema and so on sometimes, but there didn't seem to be anyone in particular.'

'Where did she meet these men?'

'I'm not sure. Evelyn always seems...seemed...at ease with everyone and didn't seem to bother about being properly introduced. Her people are...well I got the impression they weren't overly worried about that sort of thing. I think she just got talking to men at Lyon's corner houses, and so on. I don't mean deliberately. It's hard not to if one has to share a table.'

'Yes, I understand,' said Travers knowingly. 'Do you think she'd talk to men on the Underground?'

'I doubt it,' said Clarice. 'That's a sort of unwritten rule in London, isn't it? Even the most ardent suitor wouldn't attempt to make love to a strange girl on the tube.'

Travers smiled grimly but made no further comment on

that particular observation.

'Nobody came to the house?' he asked.

'No. Mrs Sibley – that's the landlady – doesn't like that sort of thing.'

'Had she ever stayed out late before?'

'No, I don't think so. Not past eleven at any rate, as that's when Mrs Sibley locks the front door. We always used to say good night to each other.'

'I see. And how did she get on with the other, ah, residents, or boarders, where you live?'

'Both of us are a lot younger than the others. There was never much socialising other than the bare minimum over meals and so on. I'm sorry, I'm really not being much use, am I?'

Clarice's voice cracked. She felt that she was about to cry at any moment, but forced the sensation down.

'You're being most helpful,' said Travers reassuringly. 'Drink your tea while it's hot.'

Clarice sipped her drink, and sensed her composure returning.

'That's better, eh?' said Travers. 'Now then. So Evelyn didn't have a boy-friend that we know of. But did she ever speak of anyone in her past, a young man perhaps, with whom she'd had a falling-out? Someone who "jilted" her, as they say.'

'I can't think of anything, except…' Clarice stopped, feeling a slight sense of betrayal about what she was going to say. But then she recalled that Evelyn was dead, and that such niceties were foolish.

'Yes?' enquired Travers cautiously.

'This is all confidential, isn't it?'

'Of course,' said the Inspector. 'Unless something comes to court, but let's not worry about that just for the present. Go on.'

'Well…Evelyn did say something odd about one of the men in the hotel.'

'Where you live, you mean?'

'Yes. She said this man, he's, well, more or less our age I suppose, perhaps a little older. But she said, it sounds silly really, that he wasn't safe in taxis.'

Travers raised another official eyebrow, this time at a more obvious angle.

'Oh yes? Forgive me for sounding indelicate, but had he, ah, made advances towards her?'

'I honestly don't know. Evelyn didn't say as much. But she sort of…warned me off, I suppose. I don't want to get him into trouble.'

'He won't get into trouble if he hasn't done anything he oughtn't. What's his name?'

'Cliff Thornley.'

'Occupation?'

'He's some sort of writer. Of what, I am not entirely sure.'

'I see.'

This time both of Travers' eyebrows were raised, and he made a number of notes in his pocketbook.

'I think, Miss Thompson, that I shall pay a visit to this private hotel of yours. What time do they serve the evening meal?'

'7.30 sharp. Mrs Sibley is very particular about that.'

'Yes, I thought she might be,' mused Travers. 'Very well, I'll call round about seven and have a word with the other residents. Oh, and don't mention it to them, if you please.'

'About Evelyn, you mean?'

'That'll be all over the papers by then. No, I mean don't mention I'm to pay them a visit.'

'I see, yes, very well.'

'Right then. Now, do you feel well enough to carry on

with your lessons, or would you like me to arrange for a car to take you home?'

'I'm quite all right thank you.'

'That's the spirit. Well, good day, Miss Thompson. And don't worry. We're going to find whoever did this.'

Clarice returned to her typing, ignoring the whispered questions from her fellow trainees. They had largely ignored her in the past so she saw no reason to speak to them now. Somehow, she thought, she had to get through the afternoon without breaking down.

Chapter Three

'I cannot remember anything like it in all my years here,' said Miss Grant. 'There were people killed in the Zeppelin raids of course – Carr's, the butcher's in the High Street, took a direct hit. Looting was feared, but nothing was taken presumably because it was unclear what was part of the stock and what was part of poor Mr Carr...'

Miss Grant's voice trailed off. The residents of the Lovell Private Hotel had gravitated instinctively to the sitting room as they returned home. Miss Grant and Clarice had the comfortable chairs by the window; the Stewarts sat on the shabby Chesterfield opposite. Hargrove and Cliff perched on the club fender.

Nobody had failed to hear the news of Evelyn's death, printed on the front of every London evening paper, pasted outside every newsagent's and shouted by passing newsboys, and now they huddled nervously in the draughty, fire-less room as if it were an impromptu wake.

Miss Grant had been chattering a long time, in that way that nervous people do after hearing bad news. She began to speak again, but Mrs Sibley interrupted.

'I must say Miss Grant I think you've got muddled,' said the landlady firmly. She never normally socialised with the residents, but today was an exception; she had even accepted the offer of a cigarette from Mr Stewart, 'for the shock', and she puffed on it nervously without inhaling.

'Carr's only had its window blown out and he died upstairs in bed from his heart, not that bomb,' she continued. '*That* was dropped on St Saviour's over the way, the one they had to pull down, and I should know because my sister's eldest was christened there just the day before. You can trust the Germans to bomb a church, I said. That's about their level, I said. And we never had *any* trouble from looters here, leastways not according to my brother who was a...who was quite high up in the Special Constabulary. It's not as if this is Kentish Town.'

She glared at Miss Grant, who looked doubtful, as if she had decided to concede her relative ignorance of local history.

'Perhaps you are right, Mrs Sibley,' she said. 'And we have certainly never had any murders.'

'Poor, poor Miss Parks,' said Mrs Stewart, shaking her head. 'I always said to her, "enjoy life while you're young". I say that to all young people. Time goes by so quickly, don't you agree? If only I'd...'

She buried her face in her handkerchief, and her husband ineffectually patted her on her arm.

'Courage, my dear,' he said jovially. 'It's not *your* fault. We all liked Miss Parks but wailing and gnashing of teeth won't bring her back. We need to form a plan of action.'

'Plan of action?' asked Hargrove, who up until this point had been largely silent.

'Yes, you know,' said Mr Stewart. 'Flowers. A subscription, and so on. For the girl's family.'

'An excellent idea,' piped up Miss Grant. 'Lilies. Lilies are the thing for funerals. Oh dear. They don't allow funerals for murder victims, do they? Or is that suicides? I can never remember which.'

'A very respectable sentiment, if I may say so, Mr Stewart,' said Mrs Sibley, 'but I think we should keep our distance. It doesn't do to get too involved in this sort of thing. After all, we have no idea what that young lady got up to outside this establishment. We don't want newspapermen coming round here and insinuating things.'

'Oh bother the newspapers!' exclaimed Cliff, jumping up from the fender and showering pipe ash on to the threadbare persian rug. 'A young woman's been killed and all you can think about is infamy for your sainted house.'

He hurled his newspaper down on to the floor and stalked out of the room.

'Well!' breathed Mrs Sibley. It seemed that any further words had failed her at this point.

'Never mind him Mrs S,' said Mr Stewart. 'Nervous type. Seen it in India. Some chaps go to pieces in a crisis and don't mean what they say. If anyone ought to be in a funk it's Miss Thompson here but I must say she seems to be bearing up splendidly.'

'I don't see why I ought to be in a "funk", as you put it,' said Clarice. 'I've had people fussing over me all afternoon at the college but I'm perfectly all right. And I think the best thing we can do is wait until the police speak to us and do all we can to help them.'

'The police?' said Mrs Sibley, as if she were describing a horde of Vikings. 'What on earth will they want with *us*?'

'They always start their enquiries with the, ah, nearest and dearest, I've been told,' said Clarice.

'Nearest and dearest?' exclaimed Mrs Sibley. 'It's not as if we're her *family*. She was from, where was it now, Southend-on-Sea. I must admit that gave me reservations but she seemed respectable enough. At *first*, I may say.'

Clarice could hold back no longer. 'And what's that supposed to mean?' she snapped.

Before Mrs Sibley could reply, the ancient front door bell,

the type pulled by a lever, clanged into life. Miss Grant visibly jumped, and Mrs Stewart clutched defensively at her pearls.

Vera stuck her head around the door of the lounge and said nervously 'it's the front door'm.'

'I know,' said Mrs Sibley, as if addressing a backward child. 'Kindly answer it.'

'I dursn't'm,' said Vera.

Clarice wondered at how the phrase 'I dare not, madam' could be so hideously mangled, and struggled to suppress a smile.

'What if it's newspapermen from the newspapers?' continued the domestic.

'I should think they would have more sense than to call at the *front* door,' said Mrs Sibley. 'Oh very well, I'll come with you.'

Mrs Sibley stalked out with Vera behind her; Mr Stewart and Hargrove made a token effort to rise but sat back down quickly. There was muffled conversation at the door; all the occupants of the sitting room appeared to be straining their ears to hear it.

The door was then forceably thrust open and Mrs Sibley stalked in, followed by two men. Clarice recognised Inspector Travers, who was accompanied by a younger, less confident looking colleague.

'These…gentlemen…are from the police,' said Mrs Sibley with evident distaste.

Miss Grant audibly gasped and seemed about to speak, but was cut off by the taller of the two men.

'Good evening,' he said, with cold formality. He removed his hat and gave it to Mrs Sibley, who looked at the article as if it were a soiled handkerchief.

'Vera, kindly take their hats,' she said.

Vera did as she was told and turned to leave the room.

'And their mackintoshes, if they wish,' added Mrs Sibley.

'Thank you but that won't be necessary madam,' said the Inspector. 'It's a little chilly in here.'

'I dare say we can light the fire if you require it. We do have gas laid on,' sniffed Mrs Sibley, as Vera opened the sitting room door, allowing a gust of cold air to penetrate from the hallway. 'Most of *us* don't feel the need of it at this time of year.'

'No need. We shan't be long,' said Inspector Travers.

'Very well then. I shall attend to the evening meal,' said Mrs Sibley. 'We serve dinner at 7.30 sharp.'

'Thank you,' said Inspector Travers. 'But I shall want to speak to you and the other servant in a moment.'

Mrs Sibley bridled at her designation; Clarice suspected she did not have the courage to openly answer back an officer of the law. Instead, she bowed curtly, and retreated into the hallway.

The Inspector introduced himself and the other man, Detective Sergeant Hollis. He then unbuttoned his mackintosh and put his hands in his trouser pockets; for a few moments he said nothing but strolled around the room, looking around as if he were visiting a country church. Hollis stood by the door, impassive.

Finally he came to a stop in the window bay; the last of the autumnal sun glimmered behind the houses on other side of the street, and then was gone, leaving the street, and the room itself in misty gloom.

'I won't take up too much of your time,' he said, finally. 'I expect you'll all be wanting your supper.'

'I really don't think we have anything to tell you, ah, Inspector,' blurted Mrs Stewart. 'You see, none of us really knew Miss Parks….'

She was cut off by the raised hand of Inspector Travers;

the signal was as authoritative as that of a constable on traffic duty.

'The sooner I have a little chat with all of you,' said the Inspector, 'the sooner I can let you alone. You may well think you didn't know the deceased, madam, but in my experience people living under the same roof often know a lot more about their neighbours than they realise.'

'Well I'm as hungry as a horse,' said Mr Stewart, 'so I agree the sooner we tell you what we know the better. Fire away.'

'I'll speak to you individually, sir,' said the Inspector. 'I take it there's a dining room nearby? Perhaps you wouldn't mind going and sitting in there, and Sergeant Hollis here will call you in one by one. Now then, we'll start with, let's see, we'll start with whoever lives at the top of the house and work our way down, shall we?'

'That will mean starting with Mr Thorley,' said Miss Grant querulously. 'But he has gone up to his room. In the attic. He had a disagreement with Mrs Sibley and...'

'Yes, thank you madam,' interjected Inspector Travers. 'Go and knock on his door, Hollis. In fact knock on all the doors, just in case we've missed someone.'

'Sir,' said Hollis crisply, and left the room.

'We're all here,' said Hargrove. 'That is, all the residents are here.'

'That's as maybe,' said the Inspector. 'But one never quite knows who's in houses like this, does one? All sorts coming in and out. Coalmen, milkmen and the like. Chaps fixing things in rooms, and that sort of thing.'

'Don't you need an, ah, what is it called, a search warrant?' said Miss Grant, with a nervous smile. 'To go looking around private rooms, I mean?'

'Forgive me madam,' said the Inspector with a deference that clearly impressed the elderly lady, 'but Sergeant

Hollis has not been asked to look around any private rooms. I told him to knock on all the doors of the rooms. I didn't instruct him to enter them uninvited.'

'I see,' said Miss Grant doubtfully. 'Well that's all right then.'

'Good,' said the Inspector. 'Well then, while Sergeant Hollis is fetching this Mr, ah, Thorley, perhaps you'd all go into the dining room and return in order, those from the highest floors first.'

'I'm down the corridor from Thorley,' said Hargrove. 'So I may as well stay put.'

The other residents slowly left the sitting room and filed into the dining room.

Inspector Travers looked down at the man sitting on the club fender and smiled.

'Cigarette?' he asked, holding out his case.

'Prefer a pipe,' said Hargrove.

'Be my guest,' said Travers, as he lit a cigarette. 'I used to like a pipe myself, but since I started at the Yard I never seem to have the time to enjoy one.'

'Dinner in a few minutes,' said Hargrove. 'Think I'll wait.'

'Don't mind me writing a few things down,' said Travers as he took out a notebook. 'Awful lot to remember in cases like this. Name?'

'John Hargrove.'

'Occupation?'

'Independent.'

'Lucky man. You must do something to occupy your time, though.'

'I have a number of business interests. Directorships, that sort of thing.'

'I see. Married?'

'No.'

'Ever *been* married?'

'Never.'

'Same here. We bachelors appreciate our freedom, eh?'

There was a pause; Hargrove continued to look at the Inspector with an impassive stare.

'Ever take the Hampstead tube?' asked the policeman.

'From time to time,' replied Hargrove. 'It can be quicker into town than a cab sometimes.'

'Knew the girl well?' asked Travers suddenly.

'Girl?'

'Miss Parks.'

'Oh. Not at all. Nodded at her on the way up the stairs, that's about all. Can't remember ever speaking to her.'

'Nice looking, though, wasn't she?'

'I honestly couldn't say I'd noticed anything about her. Other than that she must have been half my age.'

'Yes, I suppose so,' continued the Inspector. 'What about the other one?'

'Other what?'

'Girl. Miss, ah, Thompson. The one with the spectacles. Pretty too, in a different sort of way. Not quite as…glamorous.'

'Can't say I've ever said much to her either. One doesn't, in this place. It's not a social club.'

'Yes, yes of course,' said the Inspector affably. 'Oh, by the way, where were you last night between 10.30 and 11.30 pm?'

He fixed Hargrove's eye, a smile still on his face, but the man stared back as silently as a sphinx.

'I was wondering when you were going to ask that,' he

replied finally. 'I was up the road at the Maybush.'

'Forgive me sir, I'm not overly familiar with this part of London. That's a public house, I assume?'

'Yes. Off Heath Street.'

'What time did you go home?'

'I...look here, this is a bit awkward.'

'Why's that, sir?'

'Well you see, it was after hours. A lock-in, they call it.'

'After closing time, you mean?'

'That's right. I left around 11.30pm. They won't get into trouble, will they?'

'Let's call it a private party, shall we? These things happen,' said Travers. 'I'm partial to a pint myself so I shan't judge. Do a good drop, there, do they?'

'Not bad. I prefer whisky myself.'

'Ah. The wine of Scotland, eh? Perhaps I'll look in there one of these days. Know you well there, do they?'

'I expect so. I'm in there quite often. You can hardly expect me to hang around this place longer than necessary.'

'I think I can understand that. Gets rather lonely, I imagine.'

'I rather think that's the price of freedom in one's personal life,' said Hargrove slowly.

'Well, you've been very helpful sir,' said the Inspector briskly. 'I think I can hear my sergeant outside the door, so I shan't keep you any longer.'

'Thanks.'

'Don't mention it.'

Hargrove got up to leave the room. The Inspector gently stubbed out his cigarette in a large Benares brass ashtray on a sidetable, and moved to open the door.

'Oh just one more thing,' he said rapidly. 'If I ask at this Maybush place about you and Miss Parks they'll remember you both, I suppose?'

Hargrove looked surprised for a moment, then regained his impassive calm.

'Why should they?' he answered. 'I've never been in there with the poor girl, nor anywhere else for that matter. They're likely to remember *me*, I should think. Now, if you'll excuse me…'

'Of course sir,' said the Inspector with a smile. 'I must have been getting muddled. We've been on this case non-stop since last night. That'll be all.'

Hargrove left the room, closing the door behind him. The room was now in semi-darkness and Inspector Travers clicked on the standard lamp, with a small handwritten sign pinned to the shade, which read 'not to be lit during daylight hours.'

He thought in silence for a moment; his musing was then interrupted by the sound of loud protest from without the door. It burst open and Travers saw a tall, wild-haired young man enter.

'Sorry sir, he just barged in…' began Sergeant Hollis, but he was cut off by the young man.

'Look here,' said the man to Travers, ignoring the underling, 'you're this fellow's superior, aren't you? I've a mind to make a formal complaint.'

'I'm sure Sergeant Hollis meant no harm,' said the Inspector. 'Let's try to keep things civil, shall we, Mr…?'

'Thorley, Cliff Thorley,' replied the man. He angrily shovelled tobacco from a dirty oil-cloth pouch into an equally dirty pipe, and clamped his teeth down on it.

'Yes, do smoke, sir,' said Inspector Travers. 'Helps calms the nerves.'

'Damn it, my nerves don't need calming,' said Cliff, as he lit his pipe, causing great clouds of smoke to rise up like those from a steam train getting underway. 'This man of yours came barging into my room unannounced without so much as a "by your leave" and then started poking around.'

'This true, Hollis?' asked the Inspector.

'Look here sir, I didn't mean any harm, my intentions were entirely…'

'The road to a certain hot place,' interrupted Inspector Travers, 'is paved with good intentions. Next time knock and wait, eh?'

'Sir,' replied Hollis sullenly. He retreated to the door and drew out his notebook and pencil.

'Now then Mr Thorley,' said the Inspector, 'I hope that's put us on a good footing again. I'm sure you'd like to do your best to help us catch the person responsible for Miss Parks' death.'

'Of course,' said Cliff, now visibly calmer. 'Whatever I can. Shocking business.'

'Indeed. Did you know the young lady well?'

'Not particularly. We exchanged pleasantries but that was about all.'

'You didn't ever invite her on outings, to the cinema, or a walk in the park, or that sort of thing?'

'Just exactly what are you implying?' asked Cliff defensively.

'I'm not implying anything,' said the Inspector. 'You seem to be inferring something, though. Why's that?'

'Look here,' began Cliff angrily, and then became calmer again. 'I'm sorry. I realise you're just doing your job. But it's been a bit of a shock for all of us, I think.'

'Quite understandable, sir,' said Travers. 'What's your line of work, by the way?'

'I'm a writer.'

'For the newspapers?'

'Yes, from time to time. I'm a sort of gun for hire if you

like. Although under the circumstances that's perhaps not the best analogy.'

'Miss Parks was strangled, sir. We don't think a gun was involved.'

'I didn't mean…'

'I know what you didn't mean, sir. Forgive my attempt at levity. Now then, can you think of anyone who might have wanted to harm Miss Parks?'

'I really have no idea.'

'Any gentlemen friends you might know of, perhaps? Jealous types, and so on?'

'Not that I know of. We really don't pry into each other's business in this place, Inspector.'

'Everybody here got on with her, then?'

'As well as someone like that could get on with the types living here.'

'Someone like what, sir?'

'You know. Young, pretty. Outgoing sort. Goes out dancing, and that sort of thing. That's rather frowned on here. As of course was Miss Parks' background. Her people are in business in a small way out in Essex, they run a shop or something.'

'Newsagent's,' said Sergeant Hollis, not looking up from his notebook.

'Is it?' replied Cliff. 'At any rate, that was enough to damn her in the eyes of Mrs Sibley. She likes to think her residents are too good to be "in trade", as she puts it. All rather old fashioned. They're practically still in mourning for Queen Victoria here.'

'I see,' said the Inspector. 'Now you'll appreciate this is just a formality, but where were you between 10.30 and 11.30pm last night?'

'I…I was out walking,' said Cliff. He looked down and began fiddling with his pipe, which appeared to have gone out.

'Out where?' asked the Inspector.

'Oh, here and there.'

'Go to a pub, did you?'

'Good heavens, I can't afford pubs. I can barely stretch to a haircut.'

To illustrate his point, Cliff pushed back his mop of hair with his hand, giving him the semblance of a respectable appearance.

'Anyone see you?' continued the Inspector.

'I daresay somebody might remember me in the late grocer's on Heath Street. I, ah, I bought a box of matches. I then had a walk up and down the hill, or rather, down and then up. I find it helps me digest the rather stodgy food we get here, and keeps me from having to make polite conversation with the other residents.'

'Go anywhere near Brent last night?'

'Brent? Who's he?'

'It's a place, not a person, sir. One of those suburbs along the Morden-Edgware line, on the tube.'

'Oh, there. Why would I…oh, I see. Where Miss Parks got on. If you mean did I strangle her on the tube, the answer is a definite negative. Satisfied?'

'I think so, sir. But I might need to check a few more details later, so don't go disappearing off abroad, eh?'

'Chance would be a fine thing,' said Cliff. 'I'd be lucky to afford a visit to Southend, let alone abroad.'

'Very well, that will be all, sir,' said the Inspector. 'By the way, who lodges on the floor below you?'

'That would be the Stewarts,' said Cliff. 'Or the Rajah and Rani, as I call them. They have the big room at the front, then Miss Parks and Miss Thompson have two smaller ones at the back. Then Mrs Sibley, Vera the skivvy, and Old Ma Grant are on the ground floor.'

'Very well. Ask Mr and Mrs Stewart to come in, would you?'

'Of course,' said Cliff, as he knocked his pipe out into the ashtray. 'Oh, and, ah, sorry about blowing off steam earlier.'

'No offence taken, sir,' said Travers, with a fixed smile on his face. 'Eh, Sergeant?' he continued, in Hollis' direction.

'Least said, soonest mended,' said the sergeant in a tone which suggested reluctance.

Cliff left the room and the two men exchanged glances.

'Half a mo, sir,' said Hollis suddenly. 'How did he know she…'

The Inspector silenced him with a finger-to-the-lips gesture, then opened the door.

'Mr and Mrs Stewart,' he said. 'Do come in.'

'Thank you Inspector,' said Mrs Stewart, as she bustled in with her husband behind her. The pair sat down on the Chesterfield sofa as before, and looked at the two policemen expectantly.

'I must say it's reassuring to know the police are on the trail of the killer already,' said Stewart. 'Has there been an arrest?'

'Not yet sir,' said Inspector Travers. 'I expect to make one soon though. I'm working on a number of theories. Perhaps we could start with where you both were last night between 10.30 and 11.30 pm.'

'Goodness, you don't possibly suspect either of us of some involvement?' asked Mrs Stewart.

'It's more to get an idea of Miss Parks' movements,' replied the Inspector. 'Whether you saw anything, heard anything etc.'

'Of course,' said Stewart. 'Well, I didn't notice anything unusual until dinner time, when Miss Parks didn't appear.

She often went out after dinner, but generally didn't miss her evening meal.'

'I see,' replied the Inspector. 'And where were you for the remainder of the evening? Did either of you go out?'

'No,' said Mrs Stewart. 'We were both in our room. We have a small wireless set, you see. When we first moved here, we offered it to Mrs Sibley for use here in the lounge, so that everybody could listen. But she didn't like the idea, even though we made it quite clear we should pay for the licence. So we sometimes retire to our room to tune in. That's what we did last night, from about, oh, nine o'clock.'

'I see,' said the Inspector. 'So you listened to the wireless for the rest of the evening until bed.'

'Oh no,' said Stewart. 'We did other things as well.'

'Other things?' asked the Inspector cautiously.

'Yes,' chipped in Mrs Stewart brightly. 'I did my mending and my husband did his crossword puzzle. You know, the newspaper word games. He loves them.'

'Ah,' replied the Inspector with relief, marvelling inwardly at anyone who had the spare time for such activities.

'And what time was lights out?'

'We were both fast asleep by, oh, it must have been eleven o'clock,' said Mrs Stewart.

'Yes, that's right,' confirmed Stewart. 'Last night was Thursday, so we listened to the news and then the dance-band on the National Programme as usual, then turned in.'

'Oh dear,' said Mrs Stewart. 'To think we were safely tucked up in bed when that poor girl was…was…'

'There there dear,' said her husband, patting her amiably on her ample tweed-clad thigh. 'There's nothing we can do for her now. Except help the police as best we can.'

'Thank you sir,' said the Inspector. 'We rely on that sort of attitude, it makes our job a lot easier. Now, what line of work are you in, Mr Stewart?'

'I'm at the Imperial Tea Company, in Mincing Lane.'

'In the City?'

'Correct. I'm chief purchasing clerk.'

'And how long have you both lived here?'

'Oh, only a few months,' said Mrs Stewart. 'I expect you're wondering what people of our sort are doing in a place like this. It's only temporary. You see we were in Bombay for several years.'

'Where the tea comes from in India, presumably?' asked the Inspector.

'The tea comes from Darjeeling,' said Stewart, 'but it gets sent off to England from Bombay. That's where I came in,' said Stewart proudly.

'It was a lovely life,' exclaimed Mrs Stewart wistfully. 'Unfortunately the climate did not agree with me and my doctors advised us to return Home. Fortunately the company was able to give my husband a job in the London office.'

'But finding a suitable house to rent is so difficult,' said Stewart. 'We've been looking for some time.'

'Not to your liking here, then?' said the Inspector. 'Don't get on with the other residents, perhaps?'

'The other residents are perfectly nice people I am sure,' said Mrs Stewart firmly, 'but not really our *sort*.'

'Did you keep cordial relations with Miss Parks?'

'Perfectly,' said Stewart, 'but you could hardly expect a young girl like that to have much to say to a pair of old sticks-in-the-mud like us. We barely knew her.'

'You didn't ever see her with any, ah, gentlemen callers, anything like that?'

'She never brought anyone to the house,' said Mrs

Stewart, 'as far as I am aware. You should ask Miss Thompson. They were friendly with each other. Oh, that poor girl!'

Stewart patted his wife's thigh again. The Inspector made a snap decision and stepped forward.

'You've been very helpful. Please don't let me keep you from your meal.'

The Stewarts stood up and after several more 'poor girl' utterances from Mrs Stewart, they were shown out.

Sergeant Hollis closed the door behind them.

'Only the other girl, the old maid, the landlady and the skivvy now sir,' he said hopefully.

Travers exhaled sharply and thrust his hands into his trouser pockets.

'I'll speak to the other girl,' he said. 'You take the other three, I daresay it's all a wild goose chase here but you never know. *Somebody* must have seen or heard something about what Miss Parks was up to last night.'

'What about that Thorley chap, sir?' said Hollis. 'He seemed particularly shirty, and how did he know about Miss Parks coming from Brent station?'

The Inspector sighed. 'That's been mentioned in all the papers today,' he said.

'Oh yes,' said Hollis. 'Of course. But what about him saying he couldn't afford to go to Southend? That's Miss Parks' home town.'

'A million Londoners go to Southend every time we get five minutes of sun,' said the Inspector. 'So don't go clutching at straws. Stick to facts.'

'Right you are, sir,' said Hollis. 'Anyway, he's one of these intellectual sorts who's not interested in girls, I'd say. Probably a …'

'No, I don't think so,' interrupted the Inspector knowingly. 'Miss Thompson suggested that rather he might be the handy type.'

'Good with tools you mean?'

'Don't be a BF. I mean handy as in wandering hands.'

'Oh.'

'Yes, "oh". But that's not a crime, not in most cases anyway. No, if anyone's rum in this place it's that Hargrove. Shifty sort, there's something not right about him. He's a cool one – didn't fall for me trying to trap him into saying he'd been to the pub with Miss Parks, but he knew that's what I meant all the same. You can see that the Stewarts fit in here, despite their protestations to the contrary, but Hargrove seems an Eton and Guards type. What's he doing in a place like this?

'Down on his luck perhaps?' asked Hollis.

'Perhaps,' mused the Inspector. 'Make a note to check his alibi at that pub, and speak to the late night grocer's on Heath Street while you're at it to rule out Thorley. Got that?'

'Sir,' affirmed Hollis as he closed his pad.

'Good,' replied the Inspector. 'You talk to Mrs Sibley, Miss Grant and the maid. Some of these servants know a lot more than you think about what goes on in places like this. I'll speak to Miss Thompson again. Blast, I almost forgot – we haven't looked at Miss Parks' room yet. Speak to Mrs S first and then get her to open up for us. But don't be too long. We've spent enough time here and I've something more important to show you.'

'Don't let me keep you from your duties, Mrs Sibley,' said Inspector Travers as he looked around Miss Parks' room. 'I expect you'll be wanting to serve supper soon.'

'Dinner,' said Mrs Sibley, with a careful emphasis on the word, 'is already late. I'll stay here, if you don't mind.'

She folded her arms and stared at the Inspector as he worked his way around the room. He suddenly felt depressed at the temporary, rootless feeling of the room, which still held a faint feminine aroma.

'Very well,' replied the policeman. 'Keep it off a bit longer if you can, I've a few more things to do here.'

'I can hardly refuse a police order, I'm sure,' said Mrs Sibley. 'I think you'll find everything present and correct. I look after my PGs.'

'PGs?'

'Paying guests. It sounds rather nicer than "boarders", I always think.'

'At any rate, I'm sure you do look after them, madam,' said Travers. 'It's a bit sparse in here though.'

'I'm sure I don't know what you mean,' said the landlady indignantly. 'She had everything she needed. A sprung mattress, clean bedlinen once a week, and a towel, and that's more than some places would provide.'

'Yes, I'm sure,' said the Inspector. 'I'm not referring to the fixtures and fittings. I mean she doesn't seem to have many personal items. A few clothes, bits of make-up and so on, but what about letters, that sort of thing?'

'It's really no business of mine,' sniffed Mrs Sibley.

'What I mean is,' said the Inspector, 'you don't provide any other storage for the residents do you? For trunks, and so on?'

'Attic storage is extra, but Miss Parks didn't avail herself of it.'

'I see. Well, thank you Mrs Sibley. I won't keep you any longer. I expect the next of kin will be along soon to collect the personal items.'

'She paid up until the end of the month, poor thing,' said

Mrs Sibley, in what appeared to be a rare moment of affectionate recollection. Then suddenly a look of concern crossed her face.'

'Here, I say, you don't expect I'll have to give back the balance, do you? To the family, I mean?'

Travers sighed. 'I really couldn't say. That would be a civil matter.'

'I hope not,' continued Mrs Sibley. 'It'll be the very devil of a job to let this room out once people find out who lived here. I don't suppose the address can be kept out of the papers…?'

'I'm sorry but that's out of my hands,' said the Inspector. Now, if you'll excuse me, I'll speak to Miss Thompson and then be on my way. Perhaps you would keep her supper warm for her?'

'I daresay,' was all that Mrs Sibley said in reply as she swept imperiously past him and rustled down the stairs. He smiled as he fancied he heard a faint creaking of Victorian stays as she moved.

He then knocked on Clarice's door and was greeted by an altogether different category of female from the landlady. The young woman had changed from the rather severe suit she had worn earlier into a plain woollen dress, the simplicity of which emphasised her slim figure, and she had removed her spectacles. He suddenly realised she was not merely pretty, but approaching what might be called beautiful.

He felt the faintest hint of a blush rising on his face, the bane of his youthful encounters with women, and forced it back down, clearing his throat awkwardly.

'I'm sorry to bother you again, miss,' he said. 'I shan't be long. I've asked Mrs Sibley to keep your food warm.'

'That's quite all right,' said Clarice. 'I don't have much of an appetite today. And I'm glad you came up. I suddenly remembered something about Evelyn that might be important.'

Chapter Four

Clarice felt a twinge of sympathy for the Inspector; he looked more tired than he had when they had first met, and his clothes had the appearance of being slept in. She suddenly thought of him alone in a similar room to hers and felt a strange sense of pity. She doubted he was married; married men seemed to exude either contentment or despair, and he exuded nothing but a blank neutrality.

'Won't you come in?' she said. 'Or perhaps I should come downstairs?'

'Ah, yes perhaps that would be better,' said the Inspector awkwardly, and Clarice fancied the man seemed a little embarrassed. He perhaps didn't think it proper to be with a strange young woman in a small bedroom, especially one in which the bed was so prominent.

Once they had entered the sitting room, Clarice sat on the sofa, took a deep breath and began speaking.

'I should have remembered it but in all the upset I completely forgot. It was so stupid of me. Evelyn told me something a few days ago. It's probably nothing, but....'

'Anything you can tell me about Miss Parks at this stage is useful,' said Travers. 'We've very little to go on at present.'

'Yes, I see. Well, I suddenly remembered whilst I was in my room just now that she told me she had seen a suspicious man on the tube.'

'When was this?'

'Do you mean when she told me, or when it happened?'

'The latter, if you please.'

'About a week ago. She'd stayed late at the college to finish a typing exercise. She said she felt someone watching her in the carriage. You know that feeling one has of being watched?'

'I think I know what you mean.'

'Yes, well that's what she said, but when she looked up there was nobody there.'

'Could she have imagined it?'

'I don't think so, she said a man was reading a newspaper nearby, the only other passenger nearby. Then she said she heard the door at the end of the carriage closing, and when she looked up the man had gone.'

'Perhaps he was just getting off. Isn't that the way out on some of the trains? It certainly was years ago.'

'No, they don't have those carriages with the doors leading to the little platform at the end any more on that line. Only the ones with sliding doors in the middle now. When one has a brother whose main topic of conversation is trains, one remembers these things. The end doors aren't supposed to be used except in emergencies.'

'Ah yes, of course,' replied the Inspector. 'So it might have been that he didn't want to be recognised, and moved into the next carriage. Did she mention anything else?'

'Only that she wondered if it was the same man who she thought was following her a few nights before. She thought she saw someone behind her while walking back from the tube, but he disappeared at the top of the road. I told her she was probably imagining things, and it didn't seem the sort of thing one could go to the police about. Oh, how stupid of me!'

'Now then, Miss Thompson, there's no need to upset yourself. As you say, it wasn't really the sort of thing the police could have done much about even if she had gone to them.'

The Inspector chuckled and leant against the club fender. 'You'd be amazed how many women come to us with tales of men watching them, and following them, and so on, and half the time it's a lot of nonsense brought on by over-active imaginations. Why, we had one old lady of eighty who thought...'

'But some of them must be genuine,' interrupted Clarice.

'Oh some are, believe you me,' replied the Inspector, suddenly becoming more serious, 'and I'll always assume a woman's telling the truth until proved otherwise. Did she say what this man looked like?'

'No, she said he was reading his paper in such a way that it covered his face. Do you think that was deliberate?'

'It might have been. Anything unusual about the parts she could see? Was he a well-dressed sort with striped trousers and a bowler hat, or a working man, in overalls perhaps?'

'I'm sorry, she didn't say. And I presume it was too dark for her to have seen anything of the man she thought was following her in the street.'

'Never mind. Was Miss Parks the nervous type, would you say? Worried about things, and what people thought of her, and so on?'

'Not at all,' said Clarice. 'In fact she seemed extraordinarily confident, almost as if she were putting it on sometimes, like an actress.'

'I see,' replied the Inspector. 'Well that's very helpful of you Miss Thompson. I shan't keep you from your supper any longer.'

Clarice stood up and the Inspector jumped to his feet.

'Oh, one more thing,' he said. 'Did Miss Parks like writing letters and diaries, and that sort of thing?'

'Not really. She was the outgoing type. She loved dancing and the pictures and so on. I don't think I ever saw her with a book, and she seemed to just scribble postcards or even use the telephone rather than write letters. Why do you ask?'

'Oh, just because there seemed to be a lack of things like that in her room. It might have been useful. I don't suppose she could have kept personal effects somewhere else, such as a locker in the college, or a tennis club, or something like that?'

'There aren't any lockers at the college, and I never heard of her taking part in games. She wouldn't have wanted to be seen with her hair out of place.'

Clarice laughed and then suddenly felt a pang of despair.

'I'm sorry I can't be of more help.'

'You've been very helpful miss,' said the Inspector kindly. 'Do let me know if you think of anything else, anything at all.'

He handed her a card. 'You can put through a telephone call to either of those numbers, any time of the day or night, if you need me. And don't you worry. We're going to catch the man who did this, and he'll hang for it.'

Inspector Travers' car moved cautiously through the darkened north London streets. The fog had rolled in again, blown up the Thames by a chill easterly wind, and it gave a yellowish, sulphurous tinge to the night. Then there was barely any light at all as the car crested the hill at Whitestone Pond and descended downwards through the gloom of Hampstead Heath, the car's transmission whining in protest at the sudden deceleration.

'Any luck with that lot?' asked the Inspector of Sergeant Hollis, who was beside him on the back seat, puffing wearily on a cigarette.

'Waste of time if you ask me, sir,' he replied. 'The usual stuff you get in these cases. Will I be the next victim, is what it mostly boils down to.'

'You can't blame them for being frightened,' said Travers. 'Nothing worth looking into then?'

'Not a stitch. How did you get on, sir?'

'Not much better. I'm keeping an eye on friend Hargrove though. Look him up, will you? Previous convictions, and so on.'

'Right you are sir.'

'And wake up. I'm putting you on days from now on.'

'Does that mean I can go home and…'

'No it does not. You can change shift tonight, not this moment.'

'Sir,' replied the sergeant wearily.

'Worth me going to Southend to see the girl's mother?' asked the Inspector.

'I don't think so sir. She didn't have much to say. Took it almost matter of fact. Nothing about any men friends, or anyone who might want to harm her.'

'Anyone looking after her? Family and so on?'

'Got a neighbour in. Son's in the navy, out at Malta. She thinks he'll probably pack it in and come home if she asks him.'

'At least she's got one child left. What about the chaps we put on interviewing the station workers up and down the line? Any word?'

'Ah, now there we did get something. Collins – that's the new chap from the Yard – spoke to the platform attendant at Golders Green earlier today. He reckons he saw the girl in the carriage when the train pulled out. The rest – ticket collectors and so on – were asleep, I reckon. No recollection of the girl or anyone else.'

'He's sure about it?'

'Well he hasn't seen a photograph – I only just got that from the mother this morning, and it's gone to the papers now – but he said a woman of her description was in the carriage. Said he remembered her because she was a good looker. The sort that turns heads. He thought she was with a man – no description – but he couldn't swear to it.'

'What about the driver and the guard on the train? Find them?'

'The chaps from Hampstead police spoke to them as well. They didn't notice anything out of the ordinary.'

'Hmm,' replied the Inspector. 'I'd rather be working out of the Yard, but it's a bit of a trek so I'm glad we've got somewhere local to perch. By the way, get men knocking on doors between the hotel and the tube station. Any suspicious characters hanging about, that sort of thing. Miss Parks was followed home once or twice, apparently.'

'Righto,' said Hollis. 'Where are we off to now, if you don't mind telling me, sir?'

'You were only here last night,' said Travers, as the car passed through large metal gates into a brick-walled yard dominated by a vast engine shed. 'Tube train depot. I want another look at that carriage.'

A few minutes later, they stood in a corner of the vast engine shed in the carriage in which Miss Parks had met her end the previous night. The line's chief supervisor, a Mr Welland, had responded to Inspector Travers' request on the telephone to meet them. A sleek, well-manicured man, he stood watching and nervously fingering his moustache a few feet away while the detectives inspected the surroundings.

'We had this lot photographed and fingerprinted last night,' said Hollis wearily. 'And the chances of finding a set of prints on fifty hand-rails used by thousands of people is a million to one shot. *If* my arithmetic is correct.'

'I know,' said the Inspector as he looked at the grey fingerprint powder still present on the metal handrails and the leather straps which hung down from the low ceiling of the carriage. 'But what I'm more concerned about is where nobody would have had cause to leave any prints. Nobody about their lawful occasions, that is.'

'I don't follow, sir.'

'Miss Parks was here when she was found, yes?' he pointed to the floor in front of a row of seats near to the end of the carriage.

'That's right,' replied Hollis.

'But Watkins – the one who found her – said there was nobody else in the carriage. Now, unless he was a contortionist, there's nowhere to hide on here.'

Travers indicated the length of the carriage with its long rows of seats.

'But the platform attendant at Golders Green – that's one stop up the line from where she was found – says she was in the carriage, and presumably alive and well, when the train left the station. So whoever killed her was either hiding in here – which seems impossible – or came in, strangled her, and left, before the train arrived at Hampstead. I reckon he used the emergency door.'

'Any chance of opening this door, sir?' asked Travers of Mr Welland, who ceased his moustache grooming and approached the two men.

'Of course,' said the supervisor smoothly. 'But you should be aware these are for emergency use only.'

'I am aware of that, sir,' said Travers patiently, 'if you

could show me how it opens, please.'

Welland was about to grasp the metal lever on the door before Travers stayed his arm.

'One moment,' he said quickly, then relaxed his grip on Welland's coat sleeves. 'Sorry, sir, I just wanted to make sure it had been dusted for prints before you touched it – and it has. Ah, and the door on the other side, as well. I must thank those men for their attention to detail. Do go on, sir.'

Welland looked slightly disapprovingly at his wrinkled coat, and opened the door. He then reached forward and opened the adjoining door, and the three men walked into the next carriage.

'Is this going to take long?' asked the supervisor. 'Only we would like to bring this carriage back into use. We are already short of stock due to some technical difficulties. If…'

'I'll let you have it back as soon as ever we can', said Travers firmly. 'A girl's dead, and that's more important to me at the moment than your technical difficulties. If you *don't* mind sir.'

'Of course,' said Welland. 'As I was saying, these doors are for emergency use only. It would be most irregular for a passenger to use them while the train is moving.'

'But a passenger *could* use them?' asked the Inspector. 'They're not kept locked, or anything like that?'

'Certainly not,' said Welland. 'They would hardly be of any use in an emergency if…'

'Yes, thank you,' said the Inspector. 'I see your point. Now, Watkins, the man at Hampstead station, said the carriage was empty when he found Miss Parks, but the chap at Golders Green said she was on the train when it left. So at some point between the two stations, our killer could have come through this door, strangled Miss Parks and then left the way he came. As you say, Sergeant, thousands of people might have left prints on the rest of the carriage but not on the handle of this interconnecting door.'

'The cleaners do tend to use those doors,' said Welland doubtfully.

'They'd be easy enough to eliminate,' said the Inspector. 'Presumably you have the same people cleaning these trains each night?'

Welland nodded.

'Right then,' continued the Inspector. 'So if you get me a list of their names and our print boys manage to find anything, we can eliminate them easily.'

'I suppose so,' said Welland.

'Hang about sir,' said Hollis. 'Watkins said he didn't see anyone in the carriage with Miss Parks, nor in the carriages on either side. So where did he go after he strangled her?'

'Hang on,' said the Inspector. 'Come outside for a minute.'

The doors of the carriage had been left open, with a bored-looking police constable left on the maintenance platform to deter anyone who might wish to go in. The three men stepped out on to the rickety wooden platform into the vastness of the engine shed, with its din of clanging metal and shouted conversation between workmen.

'This the same height as a normal platform?' asked the Inspector.

'Yes, why?' asked the supervisor.

'Hollis,' said the Inspector, 'go back on and crouch down by the seats. As if you were tying a shoelace, say.'

The sergeant duly complied, and crouched on the wooden floor of the carriage.

'How tall would you say Watkins at Hampstead is?'

called out the Inspector.

'Average, I'd say,' the sergeant shouted back. 'An inch or two shorter than you, sir.'

'Quite so,' said Travers. 'And I can see you from here, which is where a passenger waiting to get on would be likely to stand. Try lying down.'

'This floor's filthy, sir...' protested Hollis.

'Never mind that,' snapped Travers. 'Get your suit sponged and pressed later. I'll sign the chit for it.'

Hollis lay prone on the floor while Travers walked past the carriage again.

'I can still see a glimpse of you,' said the Inspector. 'Anyone of average height walking past the carriage could see you.'

'You reckon the assailant nipped through the end door into the other carriage sir?' asked Hollis. 'Then hid until the tube moved off again?'

'I can't see it,' said the Inspector. 'Too much of a risk he'd be seen – Watkins said they held the train for ten minutes while they got the girl off and there would have been all sorts of people milling around. But then where did he go? He couldn't make a run for it or someone would have seen him.'

'I don't suppose he could have climbed out, somehow?' asked Hollis of Welland. 'Through the end door, I mean, while the train was moving?'

The supervisor looked doubtful. 'He might have squeezed out on to the tracks on the opposite side of the platform I suppose, but there would have been nowhere for him to go. Once the train started moving again, he'd have been crushed to death. And if he'd come out onto the platform, why, somebody would have noticed.'

Inspector Travers looked at the end of the carriage and the narrow gap between it and its neighbour. 'But suppose he just waited in that gap, and then got back in to the carriage once it started moving? With all the fuss of getting a body out on to the platform they might not have noticed. Hollis, come here.'

The sergeant sighed. 'I think I know what you're going to ask for, sir.'

'Good man,' said the Inspector, as Hollis squeezed himself in to the narrow gap between the carriages.

'Glad I haven't got my good suit on,' he said. 'This train's got the dirt of the ages on it.'

'We ensure regular cleaning of our trains,' protested Welland. 'And that reminds me, I must insist on this train being put back into circulation with the utmost haste.'

'Yes, yes,' said Inspector Travers distractedly, as he paced up and down the wooden platform. 'You can come out now, Hollis,' he said.

The sergeant clambered out onto the platform and dusted himself down, looking expectantly at his superior.

'What was that all about, sir?' he asked.

'A little visibility test,' mused the Inspector. 'I could clearly see you in the shadows there just now. There's no chance a man could hide there without being seen.'

'Where did he go then, sir?' asked Hollis. 'The guard and the driver both said nobody got off the train. He couldn't have jumped off before the train arrived in the station, or we'd be clearing him up with a mop and bucket.'

'He must have lain down then in the next carriage,' said Travers doubtfully. 'There's a chance he wouldn't be seen, I suppose, if he kept still and nobody walked by close enough. Nobody boarded that carriage at Hampstead. Then when the train finally set off, all he had to do was pick himself up and get off at any other station down the line. Where was it terminating? Ah yes, Morden. Wherever *that* is.'

'That's an awful lot of stations, sir,' said Hollis. 'I don't fancy our chances of finding anyone who noticed anything.'

'If you've quite finished, gentlemen...' began Welland.

'We won't keep you any longer,' said the Inspector. 'Thank you for keeping the carriage out of use for so long, sir. I know it must have been trying for you.'

'The carriage?' asked Welland. 'It was all *four* carriages from the train, including the motor unit.'

'So this was the exact same train, with the carriages in the same order?' enquired the Inspector.

'Yes indeed.'

'That's a stroke of luck,' said Travers. 'Right. The place has been tested for fingerprints but Hollis, get the Hampstead chaps and any Yard boys we've got spare to go through this carriage, and the ones on either side, with a fine-toothed comb. I want every hair, match-stick, fag-end, chocolate wrapper, orange peel and newspaper lying about collected and held as evidence. Got that?'

'Sir,' replied Hollis crisply.

'But that might take hours,' protested Welland. 'They haven't even been allowed to let the cleaners on yet...'

'Think yourself lucky the Metropolitan Police is doing the cleaning for you on this occasion,' said the Inspector, as he clapped the man heartily on his shoulder. 'And I daresay they'll do a more thorough job.'

At the Lovell Villa Private Hotel there was some half-hearted discussion of the case during and after dinner, mostly instigated by Miss Grant, but nobody really seemed in a conversational mood. The sitting room was soon emptied once coffee had been drunk. Clarice retired to her room. She wondered vaguely about going to the cinema, but she disliked going on her own and now that Evie was dead, she had nobody to ask.

She kicked off her shoes and lay on her bed, fully clothed, and felt a sense of claustrophobia; the four walls of the small room seemed to close in on her and she knew that outside, there was nothing but darkness and fog.

If only it were summer! There would be sunlight, and walks on the Heath, until nine o'clock or even later. It felt impossibly far away, like the other side of the world. In fact, she reflected, it was further. Had she the money for it, a trip to the warmth of north Africa would take only a few days, but the London summer would take months to arrive.

She began thinking about Evie's death. Was there some connection with Evie's idea that she had been followed? It seemed so unlikely that anyone would actually want to kill her. Was it, perhaps, just a random act of violence, of the type one sometimes read of in the newspapers?

She heard footsteps above the ceiling; Cliff had evidently not gone out for his usual evening walk. His shoes, presumably economically soled with metal segments, sounded almost as loud as club hammers on the thin carpet, and she wished he would take them off.

She decided to use the bathroom early; there was usually a rush around ten o'clock and she so hated to have to queue simply for the basic right of washing her face and brushing her teeth. She stood up, collected her sponge bag and stepped on to the landing.

Then she smelled smoke.

It was not tobacco smoke, or the smoke of a coal fire. It smelled more like a bonfire; something like damp leaves smouldering in a garden. But surely nobody was burning leaves in a garden at this time of night, and even if they were, she reasoned, the smoke would have reached her room first. It would not be drifting downwards from the roof. She went back into her room and closed the door, wondering what she ought to do.

Perhaps the chimney was on fire, she suddenly thought. She had heard such things could happen. She heard a sudden drumming of feet on the passage above, as if someone were running. Ought she to shout 'fire'? She decided that would be melodramatic, and instead she climbed the stairs to investigate.

The smoke was coming from Cliff's room; the door was ajar and through the opening she could see a heap of papers smouldering in the little bedroom grate. Smoke was billowing everywhere except up the chimney.

'Is anyone there?' she called out cautiously.

No reply came so she stepped into the room. Then she was almost knocked off her feet by Cliff, who hurled a jugful of water over the contents of the fireplace. There was a hiss of steam and even more smoke billowed out.

'What on earth are you doing?' asked Clarice.

'I might well ask you the same damned question,' said Cliff as he stamped at the papers with his foot, causing sparks and bits of blackened paper to fly out. 'Can't anyone have privacy in this blasted place?'

'I thought there was a fire,' said Clarice. 'Didn't you know this chimney's blocked? It's the one above mine. Mrs Sibley said that's why we aren't to have fires in our rooms.'

'Dash it all, I'd forgotten,' said Cliff as he raced to the window. He lifted up the sash to its full extent and a blast of cold air entered the room.'

'You're not supposed to do that if there's a fire, the fresh air can start it up again,' warned Clarice.

'Oh bother that nonsense,' said Cliff. 'It's out now. And I'd rather prefer you were as well, if it's all the same.'

'I was only concerned for…'

'Yes, *thank* you very much,' said Cliff with barely restrained rudeness. 'It's most appreciated but really there's nothing to worry about. Would you please go, and shut the door, as I don't want old Ma Sibley up here fussing as well.'

Cliff knelt down to the little grate and began shovelling the half-burnt papers into a large brown paper bag.

Clarice felt her face flush with anger. Must he be so beastly?, she thought to herself. After all, she had only been trying to help. She turned to go, but before she did so, she caught sight of the papers. They appeared to be mainly sheets of foolscap with typewriting on them, and copious hand-written notes, with much underlining in red ink. Her eyes widened as she saw one name written in large block capitals and underlined in red ink: EVELYN PARKS.

Inspector Travers sighed and re-arranged the paperwork on his desk in his office at Scotland Yard. He tried to create some semblance of order out of the files and dossiers that had been dumped on his desk by a succession of underlings who had been in and out all day. Most had gone home now, and he checked his wrist-watch as he heard the fog-muffled chimes of Big Ben; ten o'clock. It was time for him to go home himself.

He looked around his sparse office, decorated with a few photographs from police college and his time in the army. Was there much point walking the half mile home? The office was not much different to the sitting room in his immaculate little service flat off Vincent Square, affordable only due to his lack of a wife and family.

He decided to work for a little longer. Hollis would be knocking off soon and it would round the day off nicely and help him sleep better if he could discuss the sum of the day's developments.

He looked out into the corridor and heard sounds of laughter and good-natured ribbing coming from the washroom along the hall as the men on Late Turn prepared to go home.

Hollis emerged from the room straightening his tie, and his face fell slightly as he saw Travers.

'Got a minute?' asked the Inspector.

'I was just about to go home, sir…'

'Oh. Where is it you live again?'

'Turnham Green, sir.'

'You'll catch the last bus all right?'

'Yes, should do. Might catch it off the wife as well though.'

'She should be used to your hours by now.'

'She is, but she still thinks I've got a fancy woman. As if I'd the time!'

The two men chuckled as they sat down in the office. Travers extracted his notebook from his jacket pocket and leaned back in his chair, chewing thoughtfully on the end of an indelible pencil.

'Now then, any joy with the usual suspects?' he asked hopefully.

'Not a thing, sir. They've been running them in for the last few hours but every one of them's got an alibi.'

'They would have. Checked them?'

'We're working on it, sir. But none of them really fits the bill, as you might say.'

'What do you mean by that?'

'Well sir, none of them has a history of anything similar.'

'But they've all been had up for offences against women.'

'Yes, but nothing on this level. Strangling, I mean.'

'What about that fellow, what was his name? Sort of a simpleton. The one they couldn't get for that girl that was attacked on Hampstead Heath a few months back, due to her not being able to identify him. What was his name?'

Hollis consulted his own notebook. 'You mean Franks.'

'That's the one.'

'Couldn't have been him, sir.'

'Why not?'

Hollis gave a grim smile.

'Hanged himself last week. Remorse, apparently. 'I never hurt her,' was what he wrote in his suicide note. If he'd done it a bit sooner he'd have saved the taxpayer the expense of a wasted trial.'

The Inspector sighed. 'Why don't people tell me these things? Anyway, get the case notes for that. We might need to speak to that Hampstead Heath girl. What was her name?'

'June Philpott.'

'Ah yes. Same part of London, same method. Did the fingerprint chaps come up with anything from the train?'

'Not a stitch, sir.'

'Not even partials?'

'Nothing that would stand up in court, sir. There might be hundreds of people coming in and out of that carriage before it gets cleaned. We can't even be sure the chars wipe down all the hand-rails anyway, so even if they did find a print it might be from months ago.'

'Yes, a defence barrister would make mincemeat of that,' mused the Inspector. 'Informers?'

'We're pumping them, sir, but nothing so far.'

The Inspector sighed.

'What about the police doctor's report? Please tell me that has something useful in it.'

'Ah, well, there's something there,' said Hollis. 'She was definitely strangled.'

'We know that already.'

'What I mean is, sir, the doc says whoever did it, meant to kill her. It wasn't just, say, to keep her quiet while he took her handbag. Or while he…'

'Any signs of that, according to the doctor?'

'No sir.' Hollis cleared his throat awkwardly. 'I wouldn't have thought there would have been time for an assault of that type, anyway,'

'He might have tried,' said the Inspector. 'At least the poor girl didn't have to suffer *that* particular humiliation before she died. So it's definitely murder. Anything about the finger marks on her neck?'

'They're not finger marks, sir,' said Hollis sullenly. 'He said they're consistent with a ligature of some sort – a tie or scarf perhaps – being used. It wasn't his bare hands.'

'Blast,' said Travers intensely. 'I thought at least we might be able to get something from that. Anything under her fingernails? Did she get a chance to scratch him, say?'

'Doctor says no. But he did say there were traces of fabric on her neck on the ligature marks.'

'Anything unusual? No, let me guess; they come from a tie sold in every branch of Burton's in the country.'

'Can't say. Needs to pass it to the lab chaps for further analysis.'

'Very well then. Keep on at them.'

'Sir.'

There was a moment of silence, broken only by the gentle sound of Travers tapping his pencil on a buff manila file in front of him.

'Seems to me there's two possibilities,' he said. 'One; she was the victim of someone she didn't know; she just happened to be in the wrong place at the wrong time. Two; whoever killed her knew her movements and had been planning it for some time, following her and then choosing his moment.'

'Number two makes more sense to me,' said Hollis after some consideration. 'We know she was worried about someone following her.'

'Yes,' said Travers, 'but if that was the case, why did he choose to strike on a brightly lit tube train? Why not pounce on her when she was walking home from the station, and drag her into an alley or something?'

'Perhaps...perhaps he couldn't control himself, sort of thing?' offered Hollis. 'He was following her, waiting for a good time to attack, but couldn't help himself.'

'Perhaps.'

'Could be a lunatic, sir.'

'A madman, eh? Did it because he thought she was the devil incarnate, or something? I don't like the sound of that.'

'It's been known, sir.'

'Yes, but then all bets are off and we get bogged down in theories. We can't follow something that doesn't leave a pattern. There's got to be procedure, not conjecture.'

'Ah well sir. Procedure requires manpower. Conjecture only needs a couple of men discussing something over a glass of beer. Talking of which…'

'Nothing doing,' said the Inspector, looking at his watch. 'They're closed by now. I'll let you get home in a minute. But you've got a point. We need more men. Get Cooper and, ah, the new fellow, Rawlins, off that Bermondsey job. I'll clear it with the Superintendent.'

'Sir.'

'I've decided I need a change of air, Hollis.'

'Sir?'

The Inspector was impressed with Hollis' ability to imbue that one small word with so many different meanings.

'The air of Hampstead suits me,' continued the Inspector with a deep breath. 'From now on, we shall divide our forces, and keep in touch by telephone. You are going to consider possibility number one, that it's a random attacker. You're good at getting results from the lowest of the low.'

'Thank you, sir…I think.'

'Yes, so you keep going with the informers, and the chaps who we might call our account customers. I want every alibi checked, every den of thieves and house of ill repute from here to Southend-on-Sea visited. Every nark promised a ten bob note – no, make it a quid – for information leading to etc etc etc. Someone's got to know something. Even if it's some new lunatic in town, he'll have said something to somebody.'

'Righto sir. And what will you be doing?'

'I, from the pastoral idyll of Hampstead, am going to investigate possibility number two. That Miss Parks was killed by someone who had been watching her. Perhaps someone who knew her – or lived in the same house.'

Chapter Five

The following day was Saturday, and Clarice had no classes to attend. The morning dawned bright and clear, with the fog blown westwards to dissipate in the wooded slopes of the Thames Valley, leaving only a fine gossamer mist over London.

Breakfast was served later on Saturday mornings at the Lovell Villa Private Hotel; it was a rather desultory meal at the best of times; now, with the house being in a state of unofficial mourning, it was more desultory than ever.

Very little natural daylight ever entered the heavily curtained dining room; the French doors, which were never opened, looked out onto a small, unkempt back garden with high brick walls, shaded by the towering back extensions of the neighbouring houses. Clarice felt a strong desire to get out of the room and the house altogether.

She left most of her lukewarm kipper untouched, and took only a sip of tea, then decided to leave before Cliff arrived. She knew she could not avoid him for ever, but she wanted to get things straight in her mind before she was forced to confront him.

Without returning to her room, she picked up her coat from the chair opposite and stepped out of the house into Lovell Gardens.

She walked briskly along the road, watching the light play on the leaves as they fluttered down from the London plane trees and formed a sort of golden carpet on the pavement. It was a glorious morning. Season of mists and mellow fruitfulness! Keats, she remembered, had lived not far away and she wondered if he had been inspired to write his famous poem by a similar morning.

As she walked towards Heath Street, in the direction of Boots' library, she tried to make sense of the events of the previous night. She had pondered them while in bed, but everything had merged into a sort of fever dream that made no sense. What on earth had Cliff been doing trying to burn all those papers and pictures of women, including a picture of Evelyn?

There had been a sort of formal awkwardness after the fire had been put out, and Clarice had simply uttered a hurried 'good night' and had then almost run to her room, locking the door after her. What did it all mean? Was he in some way....

'I say!'

Her thoughts were interrupted by the sound of a man's voice a few yards behind her. She looked around and almost jumped. It was him! Impossible to pretend she had not seen him. She must remain calm.

'I say, Miss Thompson!'

Cliff half ran towards her and for a terrible moment she thought he was about to attack.

'If you don't leave me alone, I shall call for a policeman!' she exclaimed hurriedly, and then wished she had not, as it sounded like something out of a cheap melodrama.

Cliff's face fell. He was, as usual, hatless and coatless, his hair unkempt, and his only concession to the chilly weather was a large hand-knitted scarf wrapped loosely around his neck.

'I only want to talk to you,' he said with exasperation.

'Have you been following me?' asked Clarice

indignantly.

'Certainly not,' he exclaimed in a hurt tone. 'I knew you usually went to Boots' library on Saturday morning so I took the opportunity to…'

'Have you been watching me, is that it? Checking my movements?'

Cliff looked at her with the face of a rejected puppy. He really was the most peculiar looking man, thought Clarice to herself. If only he would have his hair cut or at least wear a hat to cover the worst of it!

'Certainly not,' he replied. 'You've appeared at breakfast every Saturday morning for weeks with a different book from Boots' and then gone out with it and come back with another, so it doesn't take Sherlock Holmes to work out where you've been going. I think I know why you're upset. May I walk with you if I promise on boy scout's honour not to molest you?'

'I don't think that's funny. Oh, come along then if you must.'

'Jolly good. Look, about last night. Thanks awfully for helping with, ah, the ah, mess. I suppose you must be wondering what that was all about.'

'I'm sure it's no concern of mine.'

Clarice looked ahead and tried to walk as quickly as possible up the hill to where she knew there would be more people about. She still did not entirely trust the man, although there was something in his sad eyes that seemed to preclude any kind of threat.

'Allow me to explain,' said Cliff, as he easily matched Clarice's pace. She heard a strange regular creaking, flapping noise and looked down to see that a small hole had appeared in the side of one of one of his ancient shoes, exposing a bright red woollen sock. It was too absurd, and she laughed despite herself.

'Ha!' exclaimed Cliff with a grin as he looked at her face. 'That's better. I can see it all looked rather suspicious but I can assure you it isn't.'

'Oh yes?' enquired Clarice.

'Not a bit. I've been working on an article, you see. I'm hoping to have it published by one of the Sundays. About an attempted strangling of a woman on Hampstead Heath. Then poor Miss Parks was killed and that spurred me on. I've been wondering if there's a connection, and let's face it the police don't seem to have got anywhere yet so I think my theories are as good as anybody's.'

Clarice stopped walking and turned towards Cliff, who had to steady himself slightly as he juddered unexpectedly to a halt.

'Oh yes? Then why burn your notes?' she asked suspiciously.

'Because...because, oh, hang it all, I was in a funk. I supposed I panicked somewhat after that detective talked to me. The other one was in my room and he could have picked up my papers at any time.'

'If all you were doing was writing a newspaper article, I can't see what you have to worry about,' said Clarice.

'Y-es,' said Cliff slowly, 'but I get the impression they think *I* might have had something to do with Miss Parks's death. I've no idea why. That Inspector more or less suggested it. I didn't like his manner. So I'm not about to give them any more reason to think I had anything to do with it.'

'But it's not a crime to write for the newspapers, is it?'

'Ah, yes, but this article was rather, er, critical of the police's handling of the Hampstead Heath case. They charged a man with it – a backward fellow, but they couldn't make it stick and he hanged himself. I don't think they'd take too kindly to it if they read it. Could look rather bad for me.'

They had reached the top of the road now, and a row of small shops. Outside a small newsagent's, Cliff placed a gentle restraining arm on Clarice's shoulder. Rather than revulsion, she felt a strange sense of re-assurance in the gesture which she could not explain.

'Look here, I'll prove to you I had nothing to do with Evelyn's murder. I told this to the police as well. I was in this shop when they said it happened and I'll wager ten shillings they remember me.'

'I don't gamble,' said Clarice.

'Ah, a Puritan, eh?' replied Cliff. 'Well never mind. Come inside.'

He drew her into the gloom of the little shop; there was the rattle of a cracked door-bell and she caught the smell of all such establishments; a blend of newsprint ink, boiled sweets and pipe tobacco. A slatternly-looking woman sat behind the counter darning a sock, puffing on the stub of a cigarette stuck firmly on her large lower lip.

'Yus?' she asked in a bored voice.

'My dear madam,' began Cliff with considerable charm, 'may I have a box of matches? "England's Glory", if you please.'

'Penny,' said the woman, as she slapped the item onto a heap of newspapers on the counter.

'One more thing,' said Cliff as he handed over a coin. 'Would you kindly confirm that I patronised this most excellent establishment last Thursday night between the hours of 10.30 and 11.30 post meridian?'

Clarice couldn't help smiling at the way he spoke. It seemed, however, to annoy the slattern behind the counter, who angrily took the stub of her cigarette out and stabbed it into an overflowing ashtray on the counter.

'Lor, that's the second time I've been asked that. I had

the p'lice in here yesterday, and I told them the same thing. You was in 'ere just afore eleven and I remember it because I was closing up and you made me get out a box of England's Glory matches from the back 'stead of Bryant and May's which I s'pose wasn't good enough for yer.'

'"England's Glory" matches burn longer and are a farthing cheaper than messrs Bryant and May's,' said Cliff. 'I shall be pleased to furnish the manufacturers with a testimonial to that effect, if you would be kind enough to…'

This time Clarice could not restrain herself and she laughed out loud.

'I'm glad *you* think it's funny 'avin the p'lice in a respectable place of business an' me 'avin to swear my oath on the likes of 'im,' said the woman to Clarice. 'Anything else?' she demanded of Cliff.

'That will be all, thank you madam,' said Cliff with a bow.

'Satisfied?' said Cliff as they left the shop. 'The papers say Evelyn was killed around 11pm, poor soul. *Ergo*, I could not have killed her, assuming you trust the word of that harridan.'

'Oh very well,' said Clarice. Then a thought occurred to her and she blushed inwardly. Should she raise the subject? She decided she must.

'There's just one more thing,' she said, as they crossed over Heath Street in the direction of Boots'. 'Evelyn said you made advances at her.'

'I did….what?' replied Cliff in bewilderment.

'Must I spell it out?'

'My dear girl, how very Victorian you sound. No, I did not make "advances" as you say. I merely attempted to kiss her – on the cheek, I might add – because I thought, wrongly as it turned out, she was showing some interest in me. I've never been much good at that sort of thing. She politely rejected me and as the Americans say, I "took the hint".'

'Very well,' said Clarice. 'I believe you.' She realised she could well believe it. Cliff did not appear to have a predatory bone in his body, certainly not when it came to women. In fact, looking at him now, she suddenly felt protective of him, and yet, wanted to be protected by him at the same time. It was a decidedly queer sensation, and after a quick farewell, she hurried away in the direction of Boots' library.

Two-and-a-half miles away Nat Lerner sat in his study, still wearing his garish silk dressing gown despite it being almost noon. Overweight and jowly, although only in his early thirties, he sipped his tea gloomily as he looked at the morning paper with its headline of 'No trace of tube train killer'.

He then looked around at the room. It was a pleasant enough place; a miniature manor house, built around 1800 but updated with 'all mod.cons', and plenty of room for a family, should he and Leah be blessed.

The problem was they'd been married two years and with a succession of mistresses to maintain, there hadn't been much opportunity for any such blessing to occur.

He'd wanted a proper country place, out near one of the big film studios, but Leah wasn't having any of that. She wanted to be within easy motoring distance of her people in Stamford Hill, so she could swank it up and invite them over for bridge parties or Friday night dinner.

She'd always had that over him, thought Lerner. Class.

Her father owned a chain of gown shops across north London but *his* old man only had a little tailor's shop in Whitechapel. Leah's people had only agreed to the marriage after he'd cut away from the shop and by a fluke, managed to produce a talking picture, *Extortion,* for a friend of a friend, the director Arthur Bletchley. He'd always been interested in films and was a good organiser with a head for figures, which helped the film become one of the unexpected 'smash hits' of 1928.

He'd bought Mill Lodge because it wasn't too far from town, and the price was low; he was able to buy for cash. The square mile or so of farmland and woods it stood on wasn't proper countryside, but the nearby suburbs of Hendon and Finchley were nicely screened off by trees and it was a long way from the electric railway, making it unappealing to developers.

Or so Lerner thought. He soon found out why the house was cheap – the farmer who owned the surrounding land had already decided to sell up and Mill Lodge's owner had found out, but kept it quiet. A year after they moved in, the fields in front of the house were filled with three streets of mock-tudor villas with a fourth on the way.

Six months after that, the woodland at the rear was cut down and a large white block of service flats replaced it. To add insult to injury, the little muddy lane that ran along one side of the house, and which was named in the Domesday Book, was now being widened into an arterial road; soon motor cars and lorries would be thundering along it at fifty miles an hour or more.

In two short years, the pastoral idyll that had existed there for centuries was blotted out, absorbed into the ever-growing stain of London's development.

Leah was put out greatly by all this; she no longer had a 'country place' to show off and she reminded him of this –

and their lack of children – at every opportunity. He wondered if she suspected about Evie, though he was always discreet. Most of his income from *Extortion* was spent now, but he needed money, and that meant he needed another film, but getting investors was proving difficult. He could cut back on some things – 'a nip here, a tuck there' as his father was fond of saying, but he needed a good leading lady, and they cost money.

That's why his idea about Evie had been such a good one. He knew she could act – she'd spent hours larking about with him in the little flat he kept near his office in Red Lion Street, mimicking all the Hollywood stars. She had no agent so wouldn't cost much, and she was just the sort of girl that Bletchley liked. She was a risk worth taking. But Bletchley needed a decision by the end of the month, or he'd find another producer.

The trouble was, Evie had asked for something other than money as her price. Something he wasn't prepared to give her. If only, thought Lerner, she hadn't…but it was no good. Evie was dead, and he had a nasty feeling the police were going to be knocking on his door very soon.

Inspector Travers passed Sunday alone at home as usual, with the usual tedium. After a solitary lunch brought up for him from the kitchen of his service flat, he felt unable to sit still, and decided instead to take a trip on the underground railway. He took the tube out to Brent, the station at which Evelyn had boarded the train that fateful night, and then caught a train back again. Here the railway ran high above ground on an elevated section, and he watched the endless succession of suburban roofs and smoking chimneys pass by, as the hazy autumn sun sank low over Harrow-on-the-Hill and the distant blue-grey Middlesex woodlands.

After Golders Green the train went into the tunnel again with a roar of noise, and forty minutes later he was back in his Westminster flat, reflecting on what he had seen. Something, he felt, was not quite right about that journey. But he could not put his finger on what it was, and so he switched on the bars of his electric fire and sat back to listen to an evening concert on the wireless.

It was now Monday morning and Travers was pleased to be back at his temporary desk at Hampstead police station. Sergeant Hollis seemed less enthusiastic as he sat next to his superior and flicked through a pile of newspapers.

'Papers are all impatient,' said Hollis. 'They seem to think we should have caught the killer by now.'

'Let them wait,' said Travers. 'They've picked up the idea from somewhere – silly detective stories, probably – that if an arrest isn't made within 48 hours of a murder, we'll never find who did it.'

'Still, at least they've published our appeals for information,' said Hollis. 'Nice and clear for the last three days. The chaps at the Yard say the telephone hasn't stopped ringing.'

'Good,' said Travers, 'and thanks for keeping me out of that. I haven't got time to waste with cranks, and I dare say there will be many. How did the men get on with questioning people at the stations down the line?'

Hollis consulted his notebook. 'Ah, now there we did get something. After Miss Parks' body was found at 11.03pm, the train went down the line to Morden and back up again, finishing up at Golders Green depot at half past midnight. We've had posters requesting information placed at every station, and all the staff on duty that night bar one or two waifs and strays have been interviewed.'

'Anything?' asked Travers.

'Not from the staff, no,' said Hollis. 'But we've had a bit of luck with the general public. A man's come forward to say he got on to the first carriage at the next station after Hampstead – that's Belsize Park – and it was empty. Says he remembered because it was a smoking carriage and he only gets in one of those if it's empty, on account of suffering from asthma.'

'That rules out our killer hiding in the first carriage,' said Travers. 'Or the last one, because the guard was sitting there. That still leaves the two middle carriages.'

'I was coming to that, sir,' said Hollis, looking at his notes again. 'We've had another member of the public come forward, again at the next station – a lady, says she tried to get into the carriage which stopped in front of her, the one in which the murder took place.'

'Which presumably she couldn't enter,' said Travers, 'because the station master at Hampstead – Watkins – had disabled the sliding doors.'

'Correct,' said Hollis. 'This lady, a Mrs, ah, here it is, Mrs Kelly, said she was intrigued by the fact that the doors wouldn't open, and had a look through the windows.'

'And saw the carriage was empty, presumably,' said Travers.

'Correct again sir,' replied Hollis. 'So then she walked quickly to the next carriage and got in.'

'Let me guess,' said Travers. 'That one was empty too.'

'Correct, sir,' sighed Hollis.

Travers tapped a cigarette on his case then lit it, puffing

thoughtfully for a few moments.

'That means all four carriages on the train are accounted for. There wasn't any way for our killer to hide on the train and get off at a later stop. We assume Miss Parks was alive when the train left Golders Green because that witness saw her. So she was strangled at some point between there and Hampstead and somehow the killer must have got off, but if he'd tried that in the tunnel he wouldn't live to tell the tale. Therefore the question remains, how *did* he get off?'

'Isn't Golders Green station above ground?' asked Hollis. 'What if our man jumped off before the train went into the tunnel?'

'I thought that myself,' said Travers. 'Must be twenty years since I've been to that station, however. So I had a run out there yesterday. Now the witness at Golders Green, the staff man, according to Detective Constable Collins who interviewed him, says he thought he saw Miss Parks, *possibly* with a man, on the train when it left the station.

'There's only a few hundred yards of track between the station and the entrance to the tunnel. If our man started strangling Miss Parks right away, he'd only have a minute or so to finish the job, get to the end of the carriage, open the door and jump out. Now the medical report…'

Here Travers rummaged through the pile of papers on his desk and picked out a file. He attempted to read it while squinting through the plume of smoke rising from the cigarette in his mouth, then impatiently stubbed out the offending item in the ashtray next to him.

'The medical report states,' he continued, 'that it would most likely have taken three or four minutes of sustained pressure to strangle Miss Parks.'

'The damned brute…' breathed Hollis. 'It's a mystery, all right,' he continued. 'What's next then, sir?'

'Miss Parks' funeral is on Tuesday, up at Fortune Green,

off the Finchley Road. Go along, will you? I've got a court appearance, and anyway, you met the mother down in Southend so she'll remember you. Just have a look and see who turns up.'

'Right sir,' said Hollis.

'Oh and talking of Mrs Parks,' continued the Inspector, 'I had her on the telephone earlier. Says she thought a diary was missing from her daughter's effects. Know anything about that?'

'No sir. I don't recall seeing one in her room.'

Travers thought for a moment, then changed the subject. 'Find out anything about that fellow Hargrove at Bleak House?'

'What's Bleak House, sir?'

'Literary reference. Never mind. I mean the Lovell Villa Private Hotel.'

'Oh. Well, the barmaid at the Maybush pub says he was in there the night of the murder all right, but she can't swear to the exact time. Funny thing though – you asked me to check if he was listed as a company director anywhere.'

'And...?'

'He isn't. Not in any of the big London directories anyway.'

'Hmm,' replied Travers. 'Might not mean anything. These companies change directors all the time and they probably don't keep the public ones up to date. Still, keep digging. There's something I don't like about him, but if I question him again it could rouse his suspicions. He...'

Before Travers could finish he was interrupted by the telephone bell, and he picked up the instrument quickly and listened.

'Yes...very well, send her up please,' he said.

'Witness from Brent station,' said Travers, as he replaced

the receiver.

There was a gentle tapping on the door and Hollis opened it to reveal a tiny elderly lady, no taller than a girl of 12, dressed in the formal fashion of twenty years ago.

'Inspector Travers?' said the lady.

'This is Inspector Travers,' said Hollis, indicating his superior. 'I'm Detective Sergeant Hollis.'

'How do you do, gentlemen?' said the lady with a confident smile. 'I understand you require assistance.'

Travers pulled out a chair, suddenly wondering if this person was another crank. 'Won't you sit down, Mrs...?'

'Miss Jenkins,' said the lady. 'Flora Jenkins.'

'Very well, Miss Jenkins,' said Travers. 'Perhaps you would like a cup of tea?'

'Most kind, thank you,' said Miss Jenkins, 'but I do not take stimulants. The body does not require them.'

'Indeed,' said Travers, deciding not to light another cigarette. 'The desk sergeant said on the telephone you have some information about the murder of Miss Parks.'

'That is correct,' said Miss Jenkins. 'I should have come sooner, but I had not seen your appeal for assistance as I do not read the newspapers. Except, of course, the *Spiritual Science Observer*.'

Here we go, thought Travers.

'There was a call for witnesses in the newspapers,' continued Miss Jenkins, 'and this was brought to my attention after Sunday service by one of the members of my congregation, a Miss Fortnum. I attend the Church of Spiritual Science in Hendon, you see. Perhaps you know of it?'

'I can't say I do, madam,' said Travers. 'Now this information you have for us...'

'Yes, of course. I realise you are busy, so I shall be brief,' said Miss Jenkins. 'Well, you see, I attended our usual prayer meeting on Thursday evening last. We closed rather later than usual, as the Spirit was very much upon us. Mr Frean, our minister, preached wonderfully on the…'

Travers cleared his throat loudly and Miss Jenkins took the hint.

'I digress,' she said with a smile. 'I reside at Heathfield Gardens, North West Eleven, with my landlady, a Mrs Samuels, she…oh dear, I digress again…where was I? Ah yes. I take the electric railway to church meetings, you see, as it is so convenient and runs much later than the omnibus. I alighted at Brent station, and was just walking out into the forecourt when I saw a motor car pull up and two young people get out. One of them was that unfortunate young lady whose photograph appeared in the newspaper.'

'Miss Evelyn Parks?' asked Travers. 'You're sure of that?'

'Young man,' said Miss Jenkins with a firm smile, 'I may be almost eighty years of age, but there is nothing wrong with my eyesight. And the forecourt is brilliantly lit by electric light.'

'What time was this?' asked Travers.

'A little after 10.30 pm, I think,' said Miss Jenkins. 'I checked my wristwatch because Mrs Samuels is particular about bolting the front door by eleven p.m.'

'You said two people,' said Hollis, who was standing nearby Miss Jenkins. 'What about the other one?'

Miss Jenkins paused and pursed her lips thoughtfully before continuing.

'He was a young…I hesitate to say gentleman, as that word is rather open to interpretation. But he did not look to be what would have been called a gentleman in *my* day.'

'Perhaps if we just keep to objective facts, madam,' said

Travers kindly. 'It's a lot easier. For instance, how old was this man?'

'I should say about thirty,' said Miss Jenkins.

'Height?'

'That I could not say, but he did not appear much above or below the average. You see, from my perspective nearly everyone is tall.'

Travers smiled and continued. 'Was he fat, thin, average…'

'Fat,' said Miss Jenkins decisively. 'Clearly he had little control over his appetite – something that we Spiritual Scientists tend to notice. And he had something of a southern European or Levantine appearance. Forgive me, I know little of these things having never travelled abroad. Except once, when…'

'Yes, thank you Miss Jenkins,' said Travers quickly. 'What was he wearing?'

'He was rather gaudily dressed. In a…now what is the term, a suit with knee britches, rather than trousers.'

'Plus fours?' proferred Hollis.

'I think that is the term, yes,' replied Miss Jenkins. 'It was a checked tweed suit, and he wore a fawn coloured cap, of the type worn on golf courses. His clothes were new and expensive-looking, obviously so, which is the reason I hesitated to call him a gentleman.'

'I see,' said Travers. 'Did they say anything to each other?'

'That was what attracted my attention,' said Miss Jenkins. 'They were having something of an argument. I did not hear most of it – one does not like to eavesdrop – but he said "If you won't do it I'll be ruined." And she replied "that's what I want and if you don't, it's over." After that they stopped talking, presumably because they realised other people were around, and then they both went through the barrier to the trains. After that I walked out of earshot and sight of them.'

'Did he have a foreign accent, this man?' asked Hollis, who was furiously scribbling in his notebook.

'No,' said Miss Jenkins. 'He was not the most well spoken man, but he did not sound foreign. He spoke with a London accent.'

'And the car, Miss Jenkins?' asked Travers. 'I don't suppose you got a look at the number plate?'

'Young man,' replied the elderly lady, 'I do not have the first idea which part of a motor car is the "number plate". All I can tell you it was large, black, and of the type with an open top rather than enclosed.'

'Well Miss Jenkins,' said Travers, standing up, 'You've been most helpful. Sergeant Hollis will show you out.'

'I do hope I have been of some use,' said Miss Jenkins as she was shown out. 'Why, that poor girl. I have a niece of a similar age, or at least she *was* of a similar age, some twenty years ago. She married the most peculiar man from...'

Travers chuckled as the sound of Miss Jenkins chatting and Hollis politely murmuring in agreement gradually faded away down the corridor.

'Reliable witness, sir?' said Hollis after he returned a few minutes later.

'I think so,' said Travers. 'She goes on a bit.'

'I'll say. So we know Miss Parks had a row with an unknown man driving an unidentified car, a few minutes before she died. That's not much to go on.'

'It's the best clue we've had so far,' replied Travers. 'Talk to the station staff at Brent to see if they remember him, and get looking in Records for anybody known to us of his description.'

Chapter Six

'The Lord gave, and the Lord hath taken away...'

Clarice shivered and felt tears well upwards as the time-worn incantations of the funeral service were read out by the vicar as Evelyn's coffin was carried into the little Victorian Gothic chapel in Hampstead Municipal Cemetery. She had been given the morning off her studies and she noticed three of the other girls from the secretarial college were there; she did not know them by name.

Next to her were Mrs Sibley and Miss Grant; in front were Evelyn's mother, Mrs Parks, resplendent in full mourning, and one or two relations and friends from Southend. The Stewarts had apologised in advance for being unable to attend, and Hargrove had not even said whether he was coming or not. From the corner of her eye she saw a man in a belted raincoat standing near the back door; it was Detective Sergeant Hollis.

The organist struck up the first hymn, *Abide with Me*. Clarice disliked it; she had not been to many funerals but it seemed to be a staple choice and she wondered why; it was dirge-like and she found it difficult to sing.

The ragged little congregation however struggled valiantly on with the hymn, although there was some lessening of the volume after a latecomer arrived, closing the door rather noisily.

Clarice looked round to see a tall, rather handsome man

enter the chapel; he bowed discreetly to the altar then sat down in one of the pews nearby. She blinked and suddenly realised who it was – it was Cliff!

He looked completely transformed, in a dark suit, white shirt and black tie; she noticed he even carried a pair of grey gloves and a dark grey hat in his hand; and, miracle of miracles, he had had a haircut; his previously wild mop now lay flat, neatly parted on one side and kept in place with the aid of a moderate amount of brilliantine lotion. She could not help looking down at his feet, to see that he was wearing a newish pair of black boots, the toecaps highly polished in the military fashion.

He saw her looking at him and he nodded back with a slight smile, then fumbled in his hymn book and began singing the final verse of the hymn in a loud off-key voice.

The service was short; the vicar, as he admitted himself, had not known Evelyn and the sermon appeared to be a one-size-fits-all piece of work adapted to suit the occasion. Then the little party moved outside to the grave in a damp corner of the cemetery, overlooked by large terraced houses.

Miss Grant was shedding small respectable tears into a black lace handkerchief, and when the vicar got to the part about the voice from heaven and the glorious body, and the mighty working, and the subduing all things unto Himself, Clarice sobbed for a moment, then quickly regained her composure. She was being sentimental and self-indulgent, she decided; she had not known Evelyn well and it wouldn't help Mrs Parks to see people cracking up.

Mrs Sibley had graciously offered the sitting room to be used for the reception, and had produced a dusty bottle of sherry and some very small sandwiches for the occasion. Clarice sipped a very small glass of sherry and nibbled on one of the very small sandwiches as she stood next to Miss Grant, who was regaling her with stories of some of the great Victorian funerals she had attended.

'Things are not done properly these days, my dear,' she said. 'And as for this modern business of burning rather than burial...Well! The cost of the gas must be simply enormous...'

Clarice nodded and smiled but found her attention captured by the conversation between Mrs Sibley and Mrs Parks nearby. Clarice decided that Mrs Parks was the resolute type; she had been slightly red-eyed during the funeral but that was all. The atmosphere between the two women seemed frosty, as is sometimes the case when two strong women unknown to each other first meet.

'I thought there would be a bigger turnout,' sniffed Mrs Sibley. 'Of people from your part of the world, I mean, Mrs Parks.'

Mrs Parks bridled, and took a large sip of sherry. 'Most of my family are in business, Mrs Sibley, and were unable to spare the time. We had hoped to have the service at St Peter's, Westcliff-on-Sea, a very nice class of church, I always say, but the burial club...that is, the insurance company, I mean, refused to cover the cost of bringing my poor girl back home by train.'

'You can rest assured I shall keep an eye on the grave whenever I am passing the cemetery,' said Mrs Sibley magnanimously. 'Now if you'll excuse me, I must make sure Vera – that's one of the servants – is dealing with the refreshments properly.'

'You've been very kind Mrs Sibley,' Mrs Parks said as she gave the landlady a frosty glare, and then stood alone for a moment. Clarice noted that Cliff, standing by the window, seemed to have acquired the three girls from the secretarial college as admirers, and she frowned, but decided she ought to speak to Mrs Parks. She detached herself from Miss Grant and went over.

After Clarice introduced herself and offered the conventional condolences – what else could one say on such an occasion? – Mrs Parks sniffed and looked around the room.

'I must say I thought from her letters, that Evie was residing in a rather better sort of establishment,' she said.

'You're quite right that this place isn't what one would call top drawer,' agreed Clarice, 'but for Evelyn and myself, well, it's just sort of temporary. We'd both said we'd move once we were qualified and had more money coming in.'

Mrs Parks, who seemed to be pleasantly surprised by Clarice's accent and demeanour, warmed slightly. 'Yes, I suppose so,' she sighed. 'But why she had to come here to be a typist, when she could have worked in the sho…I mean, in the family business, I'll never know.'

'Oh…' said Clarice. 'How odd.'

'There's nothing odd about it. I brought her up respectable.'

'I didn't mean that,' gushed Clarice. 'I mean it's odd that you said she wrote letters. I don't recall ever seeing her doing so, or going to the post box for that matter.'

'Oh she wasn't *much* of a letter writer,' said Mrs Parks. 'I wasn't so good at writing back myself. But she was always writing in that diary of hers. I know because she used to bring it on visits home with her.'

'It will be at least something to remember her by,' said Clarice wistfully.

'No dear,' said Mrs Parks. 'I never saw sight of that diary. Mrs Sibley had Evelyn's effects sent home, but there was no diary. I even mentioned it to that policeman, what's his name now…?'

'Inspector Travers?'

'That's him. I telephoned to him. I wanted to find out what he's doing to catch the brute that...(here Mrs Parks' voice cracked, but she quickly regained her composure)...that killed her, so I can at least sleep peaceful in my bed of a night. And while I was on the line, I said to him, I said, what's happened to her diary? Was that taken in charge as evidence? He looked up a list and said there wasn't a diary.'

'Oh dear,' said Clarice uselessly.

'It wouldn't surprise me if that skivvy put it on the fire,' said Mrs Parks, nodding in the direction of Vera, who was struggling to place a sandwich on Miss Grant's plate with an over-large pair of tongs.

'Look at her,' she continued, slightly flushed now from her second glass of sherry. 'I shouldn't wonder if she's simple. It's all very well keeping servants for them as can afford them - *I* could afford to keep one I'm sure, but I don't, because I like things done properly. My goodness, is that the time? I've a train to catch. Would you excuse me, dear?'

Mrs Parks left and other members of the party began to drift away. Evelyn, recalled Clarice, had never explicitly said so, but she had alluded to the fact that she had wanted to get away from home as soon as possible. With a mother like hers, it was easy to see why.

Clarice looked up to see Cliff standing next to her.

'You haven't said a word to me,' he said. 'How are you bearing up?'

'I'm perfectly well, thank you. I didn't want to interrupt your conversation with those two from the college.'

'Oh, them,' said Cliff dismissively. 'Husband hunters, the pair of them. Once they found out I was a penniless writer, they suddenly remembered they had trams to catch.'

Clarice said nothing, but felt oddly relieved. 'Is that a new suit?' she asked casually.

'This?' asked Cliff incredulously. 'Old as the hills. I keep it in mothballs for special occasions – weddings, funerals and the like. If it looks new it is purely because you are used to seeing me in my tweeds, which are even more ancient.'

'And you've cut your hair.'

'Yes. I didn't think the Byronic curls would be very well received at a respectable suburban funeral. Terribly *bourgeois* as the literary set would say, but I still do have some regard for manners. Did you see the flatfoot at the back of the chapel?'

'The detective, you mean? Yes. I wonder what that was all about.'

'Watching reactions, I think. To see who's blubbing and who isn't, or if any odd characters turn up – or don't turn up. That sort of thing. They must be clutching at straws. Well I must get on. I'm rewriting that article that I rather stupidly attempted to burn. This time with a slightly more favourable view of our police. Cheer-oh.'

The party was well and truly over now; Vera was despatched to the kitchen to prepare the evening meal and Mrs Sibley made a show of turning off the gas fire. Miss Grant, Clarice noticed, took the last two sandwiches from the plate while Mrs Sibley had her back turned, secreted them in her handbag, and departed upstairs to her room.

Clarice lay on her bed attempting to force her brain to remember the squiggles and swirls of Pitman shorthand, but after a while she gave up and simply stared into space, her eyes losing focus until the patterns of the faded wallpaper danced and swam before them. She lost track of time, feeling as if she were both awake and asleep at the same moment. Eventually, she realised it was almost dark in the room; the fog and autumn gloom outside the window had turned to blackness and the temperature had dropped.

She shivered, and forced herself to stand up. Realising she had left her black gloves and hat on the chair, she picked them up and crossed to the wardrobe to return them to their place at the back where they would sit until the next formal occasion.

As usual the little drawer at the bottom of the wardrobe stuck as she tried to open it; the wood had warped over many years of sitting in an unheated, damp room. Clarice gently tugged at the drawer; as had happened before, a handkerchief had toppled from its pile and become jammed between the side of the drawer and the hidden wooden shelf below. She teased out the article and replaced it on the pile, then placed her gloves and hat neatly alongside and closed the drawer.

Then she stopped. A wild idea occurred to her, one of those flights of fancy one has which seem to come from nowhere. She opened the door of her room and looked out into the corridor; nobody was there. She tried the door of Evelyn's room; it was unlocked. She crept in and looked to the corner of the room and realised she was right; the wardrobe was exactly the same, down to the manufacturer's label on the inside of the door; an art-nouveau style of some thirty years previously, with machine-made carvings of flowers down the front.

She quietly opened the door and crouched down, pulling at the bottom drawer. Rather than sticking, it opened smoothly. It was completely empty, and she removed it entirely. Her eyes widened at the item concealed on the little hidden shelf at the back. It was a dark leather-bound book with a single word embossed in gold on the cover: *Diary*.

'What on earth do you think you're doing?'

A man's voice spoke from the doorway and Clarice jumped up in shock.

'I was just...' she began, then turned to see who it was. She breathed a sigh of relief when she saw it was Cliff.

He stood in the doorway, looking at her quizzically. She was slightly disappointed to see he had changed out of his good suit and was back in his old tweeds again.

'Oh, it's you,' she said. 'Must you creep up on people like that. I was just looking for...'

'Whatever it is, get it out quick,' said Cliff. 'Mrs S is on her way up and I heard her say to Vera she's doing out this room.'

Clarice was about to protest that she wasn't doing anything wrong, but then suddenly doubted herself. It wasn't exactly normal behaviour to go poking around in the rooms of murdered residents, she decided, and Mrs Sibley might not look kindly on it.

'Come along to the sitting room,' she hissed, and quickly pushed past Cliff to the staircase, pulling him by his jacket-sleeve out of the room. She heard Cliff slam the door of Evelyn's room and follow her.

Mrs Sibley, armed with a Ewbank and a feather duster, gave them a curious glance as she crossed them on the stairs, but said nothing. Once they were secreted in the sitting room, Clarice drew the curtains and turned on the standard lamp, and sat on the sofa.

Cliff sat forward on the armchair. 'Look here, what's all this about?' he asked. 'Have you found something?'

Clarice suddenly wondered if she could trust him. She

decided she had little choice. She realised it did look rather suspicious poking around in other people's rooms.

'It's Evelyn's diary,' said Clarice softly, holding up the little book. 'Mrs Parks mentioned it but said it wasn't in the box of Evelyn's effects she was given. I suddenly remembered Evelyn had the same wardrobe as mine, which has a sort of secret compartment at the bottom.'

'What on earth for?' enquired Cliff loudly.

'Shh, not so loud! I don't mean it was intentionally made to be secret,' replied Clarice, 'I mean there's just a sort of hidden shelf underneath the drawer. Anyway, it's not important. The point is I've found it and it might contain something useful.'

'Oughtn't you to go to the police?' asked Cliff, more quietly this time. 'After all, it's official evidence.'

'I suppose you're right,' said Clarice. 'But it wouldn't do any harm to have a quick read first. After all,' she added quickly, 'if there's nothing of interest in it I can save the police the trouble of reading through it.'

'Hmm, that's a nice way of salving one's conscience,' said Cliff. 'But I'm a journalist, so don't bother asking me if it's right or wrong to pry into other people's personal affairs.'

'Gosh, there's simply reams to read through,' said Clarice, flicking through the pages. 'I never thought she was the literary type. It will take me a while to finish it.'

'Very well,' said Cliff. 'But make sure you hand that over to the police. The papers aren't saying as much but reading between the lines, I don't think the 'tecs have anything to go on. Somewhere out there,' he waved in the direction of the bay window, 'there's a strangler, and if the police can't find him, they're going to need all the help they can get.'

The sitting room door opened suddenly and Clarice instinctively shoved the diary under the cushion next to her. It was Mr and Mrs Stewart.

'Ah, we're not disturbing anything I hope?' asked Mr Stewart jovially, with a confidential air.

'Yes let's leave the young people alone,' said Mrs Stewart. 'We can sit in our room until dinner time.'

'It's quite all right,' said Clarice. 'We were just going.'

She wanted to stand up but realised she would need to get the diary first. It would look awfully furtive, she decided, if she were to rummage for it among the cushions.

'Poor dear, it must have been a trying day,' said Mrs Stewart, who fussed with the tap of the gas fire. 'I'm sorry we couldn't make the funeral but hopefully we can make amends. Alec dear, have you the bottle?'

'Yes my dear,' said Mr Stewart, who produced a half-bottle of whisky from his pocket. 'Old Scots tradition. A wee dram at a funeral wake. Or a *chota peg*, as we say in India. We thought we'd dish some out before dinner to anyone who comes down.'

Mrs Stewart brought over glasses from the dusty cabinet in the corner and her husband poured out generous measures for all of them.

'Well, *slàinte*,' said Mr Stewart, downing his whisky in one.

'To absent friends,' said Mrs Stewart, raising her glass. 'I don't ever want to have to hear of another girl dying like that.' She shivered, and swallowed the contents of the glass.

'Here's how,' replied Cliff, but Clarice said nothing and simply sipped her drink, which was too strong and bitter for her taste. She felt the diary pressing against her hip, and breathed a sigh of relief when the dinner gong sounded.

Clarice hurried to bed after dinner, and sat up reading

the diary until after midnight. She felt a strange sense of intrusion into a person's private world, and almost stopped at one point, but then decided if it contained a clue, she must continue. The police would read it, she assumed, but somehow it seemed better that a friend should be the first to see it.

Evelyn wrote in small, densely packed handwriting and went into huge amounts of detail about her daily life. It was not, Clarice decided, a really readable diary, and would be of little interest to anyone else other than Evelyn herself. There were copious abbreviations, most of which Clarice was able to understand, but the frustrating thing was no full names were used; everyone was referred to by initials.

She saw nothing that could of be of interest until an entry for September which read *'To the pictures in Camden Town with CT, because he was so insistent.* (That was Cliff, realised Clarice). *'He is sweet but not my sort of chap. We took a taxi home (bliss!) and he tried to kiss me on the way, rather inexpertly. He's the brotherly type. Felt sorry for him so let him down gently.'*

Clarice put the diary down and felt the tears well in her eyes. How could she have given the police the impression that Cliff was some sort of predator, even for a moment? It just showed how dangerous the chinese-whispers of gossip could be. She read on. There was little more of interest; some amusing passages about the lechery of DG (Mr Grocott, presumably) at the secretarial college, but then another character began to be mentioned.

Clarice had no idea who this man was. Everything was couched in vague terms but it seemed she had met him at the secretarial college and was spending a lot of time with him. Clarice got the distinct impression she was rather more involved with him than she ought to be.

Then there were two disturbing entries about how Evelyn thought a man had followed her and had been watching her on the tube. It was much as she had described things to Clarice, and gave no further information as to whom Evelyn thought it might be.

The last entry for the diary mentioned the unknown new man again. *'He asked me to his house again now that the way is clear on Tuesdays. Discussed film part again. Says the next one he produces will be big. Decided to lay my stall out so to speak and discuss terms. There will be scandal, of course, but everything has its price. Intend to see him on Thursday.'*

Clarice felt curiosity and the desire for sleep fighting each other, and eventually sleep won. The last thing she recalled before oblivion overcame her was to rack her brains for anyone Evelyn might have known with the initials NL.

Clarice wandered blindly along dark corridors until she eventually realised where she was; on the platform at Hampstead underground station. It was deserted, and an empty train, glowing with an eerie light, stood beside her with its doors open. Through one of the doors she saw Evelyn. She wasn't dead, after all! She stepped forward to greet her, but then at the end of the platform she noticed a man watching her.

Then a moment later the same man was standing over Evelyn, clutching at her throat. Clarice screamed and pulled the man away, but when she looked into his face, there was nothing there but a black emptiness.

Clarice cried out and suddenly found herself in her bed. She had been dreaming, of course, but it had seemed so real. She looked at her clock and realised she had overslept, which always seemed to make her dream vividly.

She dressed hurriedly, missing breakfast. As she rushed to the front door, with her cloche hat awry on her head, she passed Cliff putting on his long scarf.

'Morning,' he said cheerfully. 'Did you find out anything from that...'

'Hush,' warned Clarice. 'Can you walk to the tube with me?'

'Certainly,' said Cliff. 'I was just going out for a constitutional anyway.' He began to drone in a poetic voice. 'The City now doth like a garment wear, the beauty of the morning...'

'Oh do be sensible,' said Clarice. 'I shall be late.'

She pulled him through the door and they walked briskly up the hill towards Heath Street.

'Well?' enquired Cliff. 'I suppose walls have ears.'

'Yes,' said Clarice. 'I didn't want Mrs Sibley finding out I'd been in Evelyn's room.'

'Good thinking. Anything of interest in the diary?'

'Not much. She mentions thinking she might have been followed, which she told me about anyway, but there's something about a man she seems to have been involved with. A film producer, perhaps. But she doesn't give names, only initials. Do you know anyone with the initials NL?'

Cliff screwed up his face in thought.

'NL? Can't say I do. Look here, she didn't mention me in that thing, did she?'

'I thought you might ask that. As a matter of fact, yes.'

Cliff took Clarice's arm as they cautiously walked through a traffic block on Heath Street.

'Am I portrayed as some sort of sex-maniac?' he asked.

Clarice blushed at the remark. 'Don't be silly. She

has…had, nothing but praise for you. You just weren't her "type", that's all.'

'Thank heavens for that,' breathed Cliff with relief as they entered the lobby of the underground station.

'In that case you'd better get that diary to the police as soon as possible.'

'Oh bother,' said Clarice, looking up at the clock above the ticket office window. She asked for a single to Camden Town and then turned to Cliff.

'I meant to do it this morning. There isn't time now. I shall have to do it later.'

'Look here, I can take it down now for you,' said Cliff. 'I've nothing better to do.'

'There's the lift,' exclaimed Clarice. 'All right, here you are,' she said, passing the diary to Cliff. 'Give it to Inspector Travers, care of Hampstead Police Station.'

'Only down the road,' said Cliff. 'I'll pop down right away. Give my love to all at the college. Don't type too hard.'

Cliff waited until Clarice disappeared behind the lift doors, then left the station. Rather than walk towards the police station, he strode off in an entirely different direction.

Chapter Seven

It was late afternoon and the bright autumn morning had given way to an overcast sky; wreathes of mist began to roll in from the Essex marshlands along the black trail of the River Thames, threatening another night of fog.

In his office in Scotland Yard, Travers had just dismissed a party of detectives and now sat disconsolately at his desk with Hollis opposite.

'Nothing, simply nothing,' said the Inspector.

'There didn't seem to be anything out of the ordinary at Miss Parks' funeral,' said Hollis. 'And I must admit I thought we'd get something with all our chaps asking questions up and down the railway line,' he continued gloomily. 'You'd think someone in a flashy golf suit and a big car would be memorable.'

'And there's nobody of that description known to us?' asked Travers.

'I've been telephoning most of the CID men in London,' said Hollis, 'and it doesn't ring any bells with them. Of course, there's probably a thousand men in London with that description but nobody that springs to mind and certainly not connected with offences against women.'

'Did you show pictures to the old girl who saw the man at Brent station, what was her name, Miss Jenkins?' asked Travers.

'Collins went over this morning with a set of the most

likely mug-shots for her to look at.'

'I don't suppose she recognised any?'

'Not at the time, so Collins left them with her to have another look at.'

Travers looked at his watch. 'Look, here's an idea. We've nothing else to go on, so let's motor up to Brent to see if Miss Jenkins has identified anyone, and on the way back we can call in at the Lovell Villa Private Hotel. I'd like another word with that Hargrove, assuming he's there. There's something I don't like about him.'

Two hours later the two detectives were standing by the fireplace in the sitting room of the Lovell Villa Private Hotel.

'Lor, I thought old Miss Jenkins would never stop,' said Hollis.

'Every single one of those pictures reminded her of some uncle or cousin,' said Travers, 'which doesn't say much for her family.'

'It was worth a try, I suppose,' said Hollis gloomily. 'Let's hope something happens with this Mr Har…'

Hollis stopped speaking as the door opened and Mrs Sibley entered.

'You're in luck,' said Mrs Sibley. 'Mr Hargrove has just returned. Though why you should be interested in speaking to any of my guests I'm sure I don't know.'

'Thank you, Mrs Sibley,' said Travers firmly. 'Show him in, would you?'

Hargrove entered the room; Mrs Sibley hovered by the door.

'You can go now, madam,' said Travers. 'Shut the door, would you?'

There was the sound of a miniscule but sharp intake of breath from the landlady, but she complied with the request.

'What's this all about?' asked Hargrove.

'I won't ask you to sit down, sir, as this won't take long,' said Travers. 'There's just a few little details I want to get straight in my mind about events on the night of Miss Parks' murder.'

'I've already told you all I know.'

'Very well sir,' said Travers, 'but I'm sure you won't mind going through things again, just so we can be crystal clear.'

He looked at his notebook. 'You say you spent the evening of the murder at the Maybush public house, is that right?'

'Yes. I've told you that. I assume one of the staff have corroborated…'

'They've been very helpful,' said Travers evasively. 'Do you go to other public houses?'

'No, I generally prefer the Maybush.'

'Any particular reason? The Three Horseshoes is nearer, I would have thought.'

'The Maybush has a wireless,' said Mr Hargrove wearily. 'There's a snug and one can listen in relative peace. I sometimes listen to the evening dance-band concert on the National Programme.'

'And that's what you were doing on the night of the murder?' asked Travers. 'Listening to a concert on the wireless.'

'I was listening to the wireless but the concert wasn't transmitted. There was some interminable political discussion instead.'

'Very well, sir,' said Travers. 'Changing the subject, you did say your income derived from directorships, didn't you? Only one has rather a lot to remember in a case like this.'

'No I did not,' said Hargrove. 'The bulk of my income is

private, but I do have some small remuneration from directorships. You asked me previously what my occupation was, not where my money came from.'

'So I did, sir,' said Travers with icy politeness. He stepped closer to Hargrove and spoke with a confidential air.

'But the thing is, Detective Sergeant Hollis here has had a look through all sorts of public records about directorships and heads of business and so on. And he can't find hide nor hair of anyone called John Hargrove. You're a rather elusive gentleman, if I may say so.'

Hargrove looked blankly at the detectives for a moment then sighed. 'These directories and so on. Where did you find them?'

'Public library,' said Hollis. 'Why?'

'I assume they were British editions?'

'Think so,' replied Hollis. 'What else would they be?'

'My directorships relate to Indian companies,' said Hargrove. 'That's probably why you didn't find my name. If you really want to see my *bona fides*…'

'Your what, sir?' asked Hollis with some alarm.

'He means proof,' interrupted Travers irritably. 'Carry on, sir.'

'Thank you. If you really wish to see proof then I suggest you consult the business secretary at India House. That's the new building in Aldwych.'

'I know where it is, sir,' said Travers. 'And thank you for confirming.'

Travers put his hands in his pockets, and affected a friendlier air. 'I must say I'm envious of you having been in India. I've never been further east than Brussels myself. What's it like?'

'I didn't say I've been to India,' said Hargrove. 'I said I have business concerns related to it.'

'So you did, sir,' said Travers apologetically.

'I don't see how all this is relevant,' replied Hargrove angrily. 'I should think you would be far better off out on the streets looking for the strangler rather than prying into the affairs of a private citizen with...'

'Now look here...' said Hollis.

'That's quite all right, Sergeant,' said Travers soothingly. 'I think Mr Hargrove has a point. We've taken up enough of his time. We'll see ourselves out, sir.'

The two detectives left Hargrove alone in the lounge. At the front door, Travers turned to Hollis and spoke *sotto voce*.

'Pop down to the kitchen, or wherever Mrs Sibley's lair is, and get Hargrove's references. He must have given her a previous address or something. I'll wait in the car.'

Up in his room, Cliff heard the sound of a car door slam and looked out of his window down on to the street below. Through the gathering mist he could make out the illuminated sign reading 'POLICE' on the top of the black saloon car, and a man in a hat and raincoat get in to join another man similarly dressed on the back seat.

What were *they* doing here, he wondered. He then cursed under his breath, remembering the diary. He had completely forgotten about it. He bounded downstairs with the diary in his hand, and opened the front door, but it was too late. The red tail light of the disappearing police car was swallowed up in the darkness. He realised he would now have to trudge about a mile through the dark to Hampstead police station to deliver it.

He went back inside to the hallway and took his scarf

down from the coat stand and began winding it around his neck. He shivered, and decided he really must get an overcoat.

He looked up to see Clarice coming through the door.

'Hello,' she said. 'Off out? It's nearly supper time.'

'Ah, yes,' he said. 'I must confess I forgot to deliver Evelyn's diary to the police like you said.'

'Not so loud,' said Clarice. 'I don't want Mrs Sibley knowing I've been in residents' rooms looking for things.'

'Sorry,' said Cliff, in a quieter voice.

'Why didn't you go straight after I left you this morning?' asked Clarice.

Cliff looked crestfallen. 'It wasn't entirely my fault,' he said. 'You see, I thought I'd better have a look through the diary to see if anything meant anything to me.'

'And did it?' asked Clarice.

'No, but I hope you're at least satisfied that I'm "safe in taxis".'

'I think I've established that by now or I wouldn't be talking to you.'

'I wasn't just reading the diary,' said Cliff quickly. 'I went to the main public library as well. To find out who NL might be. They have all sorts of directories there including some to do with films – talking pictures, and so on. The diary suggests NL is some sort of film producer. Well, I had a look – it took me an age, I can tell you – but I came up with a list of three moving picture producers in London with those initials.'

'Cliff, that's wonderful!'

Cliff felt himself blush, and showed Clarice a slip of paper with three names written on it. 'I shall hand that over to the police with the diary. If they can see I'm a proper investigative journalist and not just some hack, they may give me more "leads" in future. One has to build connections in this business. Anyway, must dash. If I run to the station now I'll make it back in time for supper.'

A few minutes later Cliff stood in Inspector Travers' makeshift office in Hampstead police station. He looked at various notices and maps pinned to the walls while the Inspector and Hollis leafed through Evelyn's diary.

'And you say you found this in Miss Parks' room,' said Travers.

'Yes, well, ah, that is to say, no,' said Cliff. 'Actually it was Miss Thompson who found it. She realised the wardrobe in Miss Parks' room was the same as hers, and wondered if there might be a similar hidden recess at the bottom. There was, and that's where she found the diary.'

'Clever girl,' said Travers.

'Bit of a rum do, poking around in other people's rooms,' said Hollis.

'The door was unlocked,' said Cliff. 'And if you fellows had searched the room properly in the first place she…'

'Yes, all right, thank you Mr Thorley,' said Travers. 'Please thank Miss Thompson for her efforts. We'll have to hold on to this as evidence. It will need to be looked over.'

'I, mean, we, Miss Thompson and I, have saved you the trouble,' said Cliff eagerly. 'We've both gone through it. There isn't anything we didn't know about already apart from a reference to a man known only by the initials NL She, Miss Parks, that is, was due to see him the night she died. He's apparently a film producer, so I did some digging in the library and came up with a list of three producers in London with those initials.'

Cliff passed the slip of paper with the names on it to Travers, with a broad grin. The grin faded slightly when he noticed neither of the two detectives were smiling back.

'Thank you, sir,' said Travers eventually, after examining the slip of paper carefully. 'I think we would have been capable of working that out ourselves in our own good time. We do have several men working on this case. Now, was there anything else?'

'Well, ah, a favour perhaps,' said Cliff.

'I don't believe we owe you any favours, sir,' said Travers, raising his eyebrow.

'But we've just saved you a deal of time looking at the diary and identifying possible suspects,' said Cliff. 'I'd like a little something in return.'

Travers sighed. 'Look here, Mr Thorley,' he said slowly. 'It's a common misconception that the police give out cash rewards to the general public for information. We don't. Now if you're hard up I suggest you…'

'I don't want money, dash it!' exclaimed Cliff angrily. 'I'd like something else. I'm a journalist, you see, and if I could have an exclusive interview with the top brass on this case – that's you of course, Inspector and your, er, assistant here, – well, that would guarantee interest from the big papers.'

Travers stood up with a clear gesture of dismissal.

'Interest from the papers, unless it is strictly on my terms, is not something I require. I'll bid you good evening now sir, as I don't want you to miss your supper.'

Cliff looked at his watch and cursed under his breath.

'A brief statement, then,' he said, pulling a notebook and pencil from his jacket pocket. 'Do you think there's a connection between the strangling of Miss Parks and the attempted strangling of June Philpott, the girl on Hampstead Heath who…'

'I said good evening, *sir*,' said Travers with a glare, and Cliff noticed an even more hostile look from Hollis; one which threatened imminent violence if he did not leave the room immediately. He admitted defeat.

'Well, cheer-oh then,' he said politely, and hurried down

the stairs to the street, feeling the gaze of the two detectives boring into his back as he left.

Back at the Lovell Villa Private Hotel, Clarice was taking off her hat and coat after Cliff had left. After hanging the items up on the rack there was a rattle at the door, and the evening post dropped on to the mat. She picked up the envelopes; one appeared to be a gas bill for Mrs Sibley, but her eye was drawn to the other envelope. In the corner were several brightly-coloured exotic stamps showing the King Emperor in his imperial crown with 'India Postage and Revenue' marked on them.

The letter was addressed to Mrs Stewart and bore a previous address, crossed through, with the address of the Lovell Villa Private Hotel written by it in a different hand.

A shadow fell across her and she looked up to see Mrs Stewart standing nearby, puffing on a cigarette in a black holder.

'Oh, it's you, Mrs Stewart,' said Clarice with relief. She seemed to be jumping at shadows all the time these days; she presumed it must be some sort of delayed shock.

'I heard the postman's knock,' said Mrs Stewart. 'But you got there before me. Did anything come for me or my husband?' she asked.

'Yes, there's a letter for you,' said Clarice, handing it over. 'From India. Such pretty stamps.'

'Yes, aren't they?' answered Mrs Stewart distractedly, and took the letter rather hurriedly, secreting it into a pocket in her cardigan. 'You ought to run along dear,' she trilled. 'The dinner gong will be going soon.'

Just as she said it, Vera emerged from the kitchen and

began arythmically banging the large Benares brass gong at the foot of the stairs.

Clarice went upstairs and washed her hands in the dark, cavernous bathroom with its huge clawfoot bath and cracked tiling. She heard footsteps and chatter on the landing and the clatter of dishes in the dining room far below, and hurriedly dried her hands.

When she emerged, she saw a shadow move in the little alcove under the stairs to the second floor. She involuntarily stepped back and gasped as a figure emerged.

'Oh, it's you, Mr Hargrove,' said Clarice. 'I'm sorry, were you waiting to use the…'

'It's quite all right, Miss, ah, Thompson,' said Hargrove gently. 'In fact it was you I was waiting for.'

'I?'

'Yes. I wanted a quick chat before dinner.'

Clarice noticed the man had a penetrating stare; the light from the dim bulb on the landing casting a bluish reflection in his eyes.

'Whatever for?' she asked.

'I know one oughtn't to eavesdrop, but I couldn't help overhearing you and Mr Thorley talking in the hallway earlier. I was in the drawing room. Or the lounge, as Mrs Sibley insists on calling it.' He chuckled, but there did not seem to be much humour in the sound.

'I see,' said Clarice, somewhat annoyed. 'What of it?'

Hargrove smiled enigmatically and produced a pipe from his jacket pocket. He looked down at the bowl and gently tamped and prodded the tobacco with his thumb.

'A word to the wise, Miss Thompson,' he said, lowering his voice to almost a whisper. 'I heard that you found a diary in poor Miss Parks' room. And that you think it might contain information pertinent to the police investigation.'

'Something along those lines,' said Clarice, trying to keep her voice steady. 'I say, I'm famished, aren't you?'

Hargrove ignored the hint.

'The diary, of course, should be handed to the police,' he said, still prodding his pipe. 'I didn't catch all of your conversation with Thorley, but is that where he went just now? To give the diary to the police?'

'Yes. Although I really don't see that it's any of your concern.'

'Of course, of course,' said Hargrove, stepping aside and gesturing for Clarice to walk down the stairs ahead of him. 'Only I shouldn't go poking around in other people's rooms. Leave that sort of thing to the police. Or come and have a chat with me about it and we can compare theories.'

Clarice realised she was glaring angrily at Hargrove, and he must have noticed it, as his voice took on a friendlier, avuncular tone.

'Bring Thorley, if you like,' he said. 'Three heads are better than one.' He chuckled again.

'Thank you but Cliff…Mr Thorley and I are quite capable of assisting the police ourselves if necessary.'

Clarice felt a strange comfort in mentioning his name. Cliff! She suddenly realised she thought of him by his Christian name now.

'I am sure you both are,' said Hargrove. 'Well, thank you for our little chat, Miss Thompson. Do go on.'

He gestured for Clarice to walk down the stairs and she did so, feeling distinctly uncomfortable as he followed her just two steps behind.

The following morning, Inspector Travers sat in his office at Scotland Yard with Sergeant Hollis. Travers had spent the previous evening reading Evelyn's diary, but had to reluctantly agree with Thorley that there did not seem to be any new leads inside except the mention of the mysterious film producer, 'NL'.

Could he be the man Evelyn was seen arguing with at Brent station? He looked down at the list of names of film producers that Thorley had given him the night before.

'What have you found out so far?' he asked the sergeant.

'I think we can narrow that list down to one man,' said Hollis. I've been telephoning all morning about it.'

'Thank heavens for the telephone,' said Travers. 'Though we'll be putting all the cobblers in London out of work if we can sit on our backsides instead of going out.'

Hollis smiled and pointed to the list. 'The first one, Nigel Lansbury, is out in Hollywood, USA, making a picture. Been there for six weeks and not expected back before Christmas.'

'What about this one, Norbert LaFontaine?' said Travers. 'With a name like that he must be up to no good.'

'I doubt it,' said Hollis. 'According to his office he's been laid up in bed following an operation for gout. Can't walk.'

'So that leaves this one,' said Travers. 'Nathaniel Lerner. British Excelsior Pictures, 26 Red Lion Street W.1. Let's pay him a visit.'

'They said he wasn't in the office today when I telephoned,' said Hollis. 'Taken the day off.'

'Well, let's go and see him at home,' said Travers. 'Where does he live?'

'His secretary wouldn't give that out over the telephone,' said Hollis glumly.

'For the Lord's sake, didn't you tell her you were a

policeman?'

'Yes,' protested Hollis, 'but she said I could be anyone. She was a saucy piece.'

'She's spent too much time amongst actors, most likely,' said Travers, 'and thinks everyone's pretending to be something they're not. Tried the phone book?'

'Yes sir, but there's four N. Lerners listed in London.'

'Right then, let's get over to his office.'

Hollis stood up and made for the coat stand as Travers followed.

'On second thoughts,' said the Inspector, 'you get over to India House. Find out if Hargrove's story about being listed there adds up.'

'Righto, sir,' said Hollis, putting on his hat and raincoat. 'What about his previous address I got off old Ma Sibley last night? Want me to check that?'

'No, it's all right, I'll have a look,' said Travers. 'I've some business to clear up at the Hampstead station anyway. Lord, I'll be pleased when we catch this chap. I'm used to a ten minute walk to work in the mornings, not a thirty minute drive.'

As it transpired, it took Travers nearly forty minutes to reach his destination. After calling at Lerner's office and extracting the man's home address from his officious secretary, he sat back in the police car as Barnes steered the vehicle at a tortuously slow pace past traffic blocks, road-works and sundry other delays. Travers tapped his fingers impatiently on the arm-rest as the car slowed to allow a crocodile of school children to cross the road at Swiss Cottage; then finally the way was clear and the car accelerated to a steady 30 miles per hour along the broad expanse of the Finchley Road.

At Golders Green Barnes had to stop to consult a street map.

'Lost already?' enquired Travers.

'I know the general lie of the land, sir,' said Barnes, 'but this sounds like a new place. Not on the map yet.'

'I'm from west London,' said Travers. 'This part of the world the maps might as well have "here be dragons" on them.'

Barnes chuckled. 'We'll find it sir.'

The car travelled on along a long parade of shops and then past large half-timbered villas set back from the road; gradually the houses began to thin out. There was a white-boarded public house, a market garden, and then nothing but trees, gleaming golden in the autumnal sunlight. Barnes slowed the car to a crawl and looked doubtfully from side to side.

'Pull over and ask this bobby,' said Travers. 'We'll be here all day otherwise.'

The white-gloved constable on point duty straightened when he saw the official car pull up.

'Mill Lodge?' he said doubtfully, repeating the driver's enquiry. 'Oh, that must be the old place by the building site down the road. Turn right here, last on the left, four hundred yards along.'

The car nosed its way gently on to a rough, unmade road lined with half-built houses until it petered out into a cart-track in front of a pleasant looking house, early Victorian or Georgian, thought Travers, though he wasn't sure.

A bored-looking servant with her lace cap askew answered the door.

'Nobody at 'ome,' she said, and tried to close the door.

Travers deftly put his foot in the door. 'I think there is, miss. Be so kind, would you?'

The girl opened her mouth to speak again but was quickly pushed aside by a fat man with receding hair dressed in a checked golfing suit.

'Yes, what do you want?' he asked brusquely. 'We don't buy things at the door, so…'

The man's eyebrows shot up as he saw PC Barnes and the black police car parked nearby.

'Mr Nathaniel Lerner?' asked Travers.

'What's this about?'

'My name's Inspector Travers, of Scotland Yard.'

'So what's that to do with me?'

'May we come in, sir? Only it's a bit noisy out here.'

Travers gestured to the houses opposite, where two men were using a large saw to cut some roof timbers while a third hammered nails into a plank.

'OK then,' said Lerner reluctantly, and showed the two men into a small study which looked out onto the garden. Barnes positioned himself by the door, and Travers could see that Lerner had noticed this.

'I'll try not to take up too much of your time, sir,' said Travers. 'May I confirm you are Nathaniel Lerner, a producer at British Excelsior Pictures?'

'S'right.'

'Very well. Were you acquainted with a young woman by the name of Evelyn Parks?'

Lerner licked his lips and patted back a strand of hair that had fallen across his forehead.

'Look, what's this got to do with me?' he asked nervously.

'It's a simple question, sir,' said Travers. 'Did you or did you not know Evelyn Parks?'

'All right, so what if I did?'

'I'll take that as an affirmative. You're aware she was murdered?'

'Course…course I am. It's been in all the papers. But you don't think I…'

'We're just eliminating certain parties from our enquiries at the moment,' said Travers. 'Where were you between 10.30 and 11.30 pm last Thursday?'

Travers noticed beads of sweat appear on the man's forehead.

'Last Thursday, let me think…last Thursday. Oh…ah, listen, man to man, this won't go any further than this room, will it?'

'I can't promise that sir. Is there something you want to tell me?'

'Well, let me think…Thursday…'

Travers could see the man was playing for time.

'Let me jog your memory, Mr Lerner,' he said brightly. 'We have a witness who says a man answering your description was at Brent station with Miss Parks at approximately 10.45 pm on Thursday. That's about 20 minutes before she was found dead on a train two stops down the line at Hampstead. What's more, this witness says the man and woman in question were arguing.'

'She's lying, she can't have…'

'Who's lying?'

'That witness. How did…'

'I didn't say it was a woman.'

All the bluster seemed to go out of Lerner like air from a balloon and he visibly sagged, putting his arm on the back of a chair for support.

'All right,' he said. 'All right, I was there. With Evie. It was that pint-sized old girl that saw us, wasn't it? Noticed she gave me a funny look at the time.'

'Come on Lerner,' said Travers. 'Let's have the full story.'

'You can't tell the wife. She'll crucify me.'

The man was almost in tears and Travers felt a wave of revulsion at this philanderer. He determined to push home his advantage.

'You should have thought of that before. Let's have it.'

'All right,' repeated Lerner. 'Evie and me were, were, what you might call very good friends. You know how it is.'

'Not really, but I can guess. And your wife didn't know about it?'

'No.'

'Where is she now? Mrs Lerner, I mean?'

'It's her bridge class in Hendon. I'll have to pick her up soon in the car.'

'What sort of car do you have?'

'Sunbeam three litre.'

'That's a tourer – an open top model, isn't it?'

'Yes. What's that got to…'

'Never mind. What happened after you went up on to the platform?'

'Look, mister, Inspector, I…'

'What happened?'

'I didn't do anything to her, honest to God, I didn't…'

Travers' patience gave out.

'Nathaniel Lerner, I am arresting you on suspicion of the murder of Evelyn Parks. Take him to the car, Barnes.'

The constable stepped forward to take Lerner's arm.

'But what about my wife's lift home from bridge?' he whined.

Travers looked at him with disgust. 'She'll have to take the tube.'

The police car pulled away with Lerner sitting nervously on the edge of the back seat next to Travers; he noticed the servant peering out from one of the downstairs windows of the house, and two workmen on the villa opposite looking on with idle curiosity.

'Don't get any ideas about running off,' said Travers.

'These doors are locked from the front.'

Lerner said nothing, but bit his lip and continued to gaze out of the window.

The car nosed its way onto a rustic gravel lane leading down a hill; at its foot a workman in a leather jerkin held up a red 'stop' sign as a mechanical digger slowly tore up the grass verge on one side.

'Going to be long?' asked Barnes to the workman.

'Sorry chum,' he said, 'it'll take at least five minutes to get that digger out of the way on this stretch. You can always take the long way round through Hendon.'

Barnes looked doubtful but Travers leaned forward. 'That won't be any quicker. Wait here,' he said. 'Let me out, but keep an eye on him.'

Barnes nodded and operated the locking mechanism, allowing the Inspector to step out of the car.

He walked along the grass verge to a small copse which ran alongside a little stream; further along the stream widened into a large mill-pond. The derelict remains of a water-mill were on the other side, and bore a large 'land acquired' sign with the name of a local house-builder underneath.

He knew there was something about this place that reminded him of something. Suddenly it all came back to him. He had been here before; before the war. When had it been, he wondered? 1908? He was still at school, so it cannot have been later than 1909. There had been a poster on the underground, he recalled, showing foggy, smoky London but beyond it a bright, sunlit arcadia that could be reached by the new electric tube.

He had been born and raised in urban London, amidst the endless stucco'd canyons of Notting Hill, and had never spent much time outside the city. He had seen that poster and wondered if such an unreal-looking place actually existed.

He remembered it all now; there had been a girl...what was her name...? A neighbour's daughter, with voluptuous, sensual features and a hobble-skirt, daringly showing an inch or two of ankle. His mother had thought her 'common'. Dorothy something. They had taken the tube to Golders Green, where the line ended in those days, and had walked for what seemed like hours across the fields until finally they had stopped here, at the mill pond.

It had been a stifling hot day and she had dared him to swim in the pond; wanting to impress her he had stripped off to his underwear and leapt in to its clear green depths; he still recalled the surprising coldness of the water on his skin and the sound of Dorothy's laughter.

Afterwards, while he dried off, they had lain in the shadow of the plane trees lining the little lane, the one he was now standing on; she, older than him by a year or so, had looked at him with a strange intensity. She was no longer laughing. A more experienced man would have understood what that look meant and perhaps taken advantage of it, but he, naive and still innocent, assumed she had become bored, and he suggested they go home. He did not recall ever seeing her again after that.

And this was the arcadia they had found...he looked down at the scummy surface of the mill pond; a few discarded tin cans and cigarette packets floated at the edge of the murky water. A large new block of flats nearby, built in the jazz-modern style, cut out much of the sunlight from the pond, and the plane trees he had lain under beside Dorothy were gone, replaced by the freshly creosoted back fences of a row of semi-detached houses.

If any birds were singing, their sound was drowned out by the chugging of the mechanical digger, tearing up the verge of the old country lane to create part of the new bypass road.

He heard the brief rasp of a klaxon, and looked round to see that the road had cleared; Barnes was waving at him. He trudged back to the car and chided himself for his sentimentality. People needed houses, and roads to get to them; better for them to be built here than for folk to be crammed into slums in the centre of London. Arcadia indeed! That world had ended in 1914, along with his youth and innocence, and there was no sense mourning it. He had a murderer to catch.

As the car climbed the steep hill at North End Road, the underground poster flashed into Travers' mind again. There was something about it...something about the journey between London and the suburbs that was bothering him.

His thoughts were interrupted by Barnes' voice as the car pulled into the yard at the rear of Hampstead police station.

'Here we are sir,' said the driver.

'Thanks. Wait here, will you? I'll get this one booked in and then come out.'

'What's going to happen?' asked Lerner with alarm. 'Where are you taking me...?'

'To a nice quiet cell,' said Travers. 'Where you can calm down and collect your thoughts. I'll be back later for a little chat.'

Chapter Eight

Once Lerner had been booked, Travers telephoned Hollis at the Yard and asked him to get to Hampstead as soon as possible. He then got Barnes to drive back the way they had come, over Whitestone Pond and down North End Road. He told the constable to park outside the Bull and Bush pub.

'Bit early, sir,' said Barnes with a grin.

'I'm after clues, not beer, worst luck' said Travers, as he slammed the car door shut. 'I'll only be two ticks.'

He consulted his notebook and reminded himself of the previous address that Hargrove had given Mrs Sibley.

North End Terrace was a small cul-de-sac, lined with Georgian houses on one side and the trees of Hampstead Heath on the other. He knocked on the door of Hargrove's former residence. An imperious looking woman with iron-grey hair opened the door and looked down at him from the step.

'Yes?'

'Good afternoon, madam. I should like to confirm that a certain person lived at this address until recently.'

'What on earth is this about?' asked the woman. 'You're not a bailiff of some sort, are you?'

'No madam, I'm a police officer.'

'Police?' gasped the woman. 'This is a respectable...'

'If I might come in for a moment,' interrupted Travers,

showing her his warrant card.

The woman reluctantly opened the door, looked from side to side along the street, then closed it firmly.

'Thank you, Mrs, ah…?'

'*Miss* Joyce-Burton,' said the woman. 'I suppose this is something to do with that poor girl that was found wandering on the Heath earlier this year. Although I had assumed that was all over and done with now. I believe another incident has occurred, a girl killed on the station at Hampstead?'

'Yes, I'm aware of those cases,' said Travers evasively. 'I'm not here to speak about them. I wish to confirm a Mr John Hargrove was a resident here.'

'*Dear* Mr Hargrove,' said Miss Joyce-Burton with some relief. 'Yes, he lived here for some months. He hasn't done anything wrong, has he?'

'I'm pursuing certain lines of enquiry, Miss Joyce-Burton,' said Travers, again evasively. 'I assume his references were satisfactory?'

'Most certainly,' said Miss Joyce-Burton. 'We do not allow tenants without letters of introduction, that is, my sister and I.'

'I see. Do you happen to have a copy of his letter of introduction?'

'It will be here somewhere, but my sister deals with that side of things. You would have to ask her, but she is presently visiting friends in Suffolk.'

'That won't be necessary just now, madam,' said Travers. 'May I see Mr Hargrove's former room?'

'Very well, the room is untenanted just now,' said the landlady, and showed Travers up a steep flight of steps to a small attic bedroom, which looked out onto the street from one window, and onto a row of little back gardens from the other.

His eye was drawn to a strange construction like a large square chimney at the end of the row of back gardens.

'What was he like, this Mr Hargrove?' he asked.

'Mr Hargrove was one of our better guests,' said Miss Joyce-Burton. 'He always paid his rent on time and was very much the class of person that one would hope to have as a tenant. In fact he was barely at home at all.'

'Oh yes? Working away, was he?'

'I don't think so...he enjoyed long walks, it seems, and was often in and out of the house at all hours. I wondered at first if he drank, but there was never any evidence of that. He...'

'What's that building there?' interrupted Travers, pointing out of the window to the strange construction he had noticed earlier. 'Some sort of factory chimney?'

'Certainly not,' sniffed Miss Joyce-Burton. 'The lease of this land specifically prohibits the carrying on of noisome trades or...'

'What is it then?' pressed Travers.

'I remember Mr Hargrove asking me exactly the same question.' replied the landlady. 'It is a ventilation shaft, I believe, for the underground railway, which runs beneath this road.'

'I see,' said Travers thoughtfully. 'Well, thank you Miss Joyce, ah...'

'Joyce-Burton,' said the woman, with something that was almost a smile. 'I am glad to hear Mr Hargrove is not in any trouble. I would be very surprised to hear he was the wrong sort. One develops an instinct for recognising good breeding as one gets older, don't you think? And of course, he was an officer and a gentleman.'

'Oh?' asked Travers. 'Did he mention military service?'

'He never mentioned anything specifically,' said Miss Joyce-Burton, 'but I recognised his tie straight away.

Indian Army. My brother served in it in the last war, and had the same tie.'

'Where is he now, your brother?'

'He was killed in Palestine, in 1917.'

'I'm sorry to hear that. You've been very helpful,' said Travers thoughtfully, and let himself out.

Twenty minutes later he was seated with Sergeant Hollis in a bleak room behind Hampstead police station, with a barred window facing a car park. Lerner, his tie and braces removed for his own protection, sat awkwardly facing the two men.

'I want a lawyer,' he said. 'I haven't done anything.'

'So you say,' said Travers. 'You can have a lawyer if you want, but if you haven't done anything, why not try to convince me here and now instead of waiting for one?

Lerner paused and licked his lips. 'All right, all right. What do you want I should tell you?'

'Good,' said Travers. 'Let's start at the beginning, shall we? How long had you known Evelyn Parks?'

'About two months,' said Lerner slowly.

'And how did you get to know her?'

'She did typing, see, at that secretarial college in Camden Town. They do a special rate for businesses, to give the girls practice, like. She used to deliver things to us at the office, copies of scripts and so on. Well, we got talking, and it turned out we had a lot in common.' He folded his arms defensively.

'Oh yes, such as what?' asked Travers.

'She liked films. She'd seen the one I produced, *Extortion*, and she liked it.'

'I saw that one, sir,' said Hollis. 'Wasn't bad.'

'Yes, thank you Hollis,' said Travers. 'And so you started up a love affair, is that it?'

'If you want to call it that.'

'And your wife didn't know?'

'Course she didn't.'

'What were you arguing about the night she died?'

'We were...look, it sounds bad, I know...'

'Indeed it does, Mr Lerner. What was the subject of your argument?'

'She...she sprung something on me and it made me lose my temper.'

'Oh yes? In the family way, was she?'

'Course not. Do I look stupid?'

'Let's get to the point then.'

'She wanted me to divorce my wife and marry her.'

'And you said no?'

'What do you think? We're not in Hollywood where they divorce at the drop of a hat. It would be the ruin of me. It was only luck she turned up on the doorstep when my wife was out at her bridge night.'

'Why not just call the whole thing off, then? Ships that pass in the night, and all that. She had no hold on you.'

Lerner leaned forward with an angry expression on his face. 'Because we had an agreement, see. I'd offered her the lead part in my next picture.'

'She was studying typing, not acting.'

'Yes, but I could tell she had talent and she gave a good screen test. Bletchley – that's Arthur Bletchley, the director, you know – saw it and liked her too. Best thing was she was asking a fraction of what most of the actresses expect, just pocket money really, and she had no agent to take a cut either.'

'And so she made her offer to be in your next picture conditional on a divorce, is that it?'

'You've got it in one,' said Lerner. 'I wasn't putting up with that sort of blackmail, and I told her straight. If she pulled out, it meant I'd probably lose the picture. That's a dead cert now, of course.'

'So you got on the train at Brent, and what then?'

'We had a, let's call it a heated discussion. At Golders Green I said to myself I wasn't getting anywhere, so I got off the train and took a cab back to Brent, then drove home.'

Travers frowned. This last revelation put a new slant on things.

'Get the badge number of the cabbie, did you?'

'Talk sense. I never even saw his face.'

'But he'd be able to identify you, if we can find him?'

'I don't know, do I? Here, you mean if he can't…then…'

Travers sat back and folded his arms, looking the perspiring man opposite squarely in the face.

'Then you're in very deep trouble, Mr Lerner.'

The week passed in a blur for Clarice; she immersed herself in her studies, trying to avoid the conversations in the dining room about Evelyn's murder. The consensus among the residents seemed to be that the police were not doing enough to catch the killer. This reflected the general tone of the newspapers, which were becoming impatient for new revelations in the case.

By the time Saturday arrived, Clarice felt she could contain her claustrophobia no more. She had to get out; the weather was unusually pleasant and she was utterly sick of the constraints of the Lovell Villa Private Hotel.

'Going out?' asked Cliff after breakfast, as he passed Clarice in the hall. She already wore her walking shoes and was putting on her mackintosh.

'I thought I'd go for a walk over the Heath,' she said,

then after a moment's hesitation, added 'like to come along?'

'I'll say,' replied Cliff enthusiastically. 'I've been cooped up in that room with that typewriter all week.'

'Haven't you sold your article yet?' asked Clarice as they stepped out of the front door.

'No such luck,' frowned Cliff. 'The *Sketch* says it's too highbrow for them, and the *Times* says it's too lowbrow. I think the real problem is there's nothing new to say in the case.'

'I suppose these things take time,' said Clarice, 'but the police really don't seem to be getting anywhere, do they?'

'Look here, do you really want to walk?' asked Cliff. 'Or would you prefer a ride on the Brough?'

'What on earth do you mean?' asked Clarice.

'My motorcycle, I mean. A Brough Superior. The one I keep in the garage.'

He nodded to the little prefabricated garage on the far side of the garden that housed Mr Stewart's motor-car.

'Why not?' said Clarice. 'It sounds rather thrilling.'

'Come one then,' said Cliff, then stopped. 'Blast, I forgot. She's almost out of petrol and I haven't a sou left to buy any with.'

'You're not supposed to tell me that until we actually do run out of petrol, miles from anywhere,' joked Clarice.

Cliff looked confused, then smiled. 'What a sewer of a mind you have, Miss Thompson. Anyway, that old running out of petrol trick only works with motor cars. Come on, a walk will do us both good.'

Before long they had passed through the bustle of Hampstead High Street and were on a gravel path winding its way through the sandy hills of the Heath. Eventually they reached the highest point of the parkland, where children flew kites and the vastness of London spread out before them, the view stretching as far as the blue-green shelf of the North Downs.

'Isn't it splendid!' exclaimed Clarice, as she collapsed on a bench facing the view. 'Not the least sign of that beastly fog. It's almost as if it were summer. Aren't you going to sit down, Mr Thorley?'

Cliff sat awkwardly beside her on the bench, and began filling his pipe. He lit it and seemed to relax somewhat as he puffed away. The open air suited him, she decided. Somehow his decaying tweeds and ancient shoes went better with the rugged landscape of the Heath than the rooms of a suburban boarding house .

'I say...' began Clarice.

'Look here...' said Cliff at the same moment.

Clarice laughed. 'You go first.'

'I was going to say,' replied Cliff, 'now that we're friends, I hope, you might use my Christian name.'

'Isn't that odd,' said Clarice. 'I was about to say exactly the same thing. Come along then, "Cliff",' she added, standing up. 'It doesn't do to sit too long on a walk or one's legs become less co-operative.'

They stood up and for a brief moment she held his arm as they stepped over the tussocky ground to the path. She sensed more awkwardness, and stepped away from him.

'What do you think of Mr Hargrove?' she asked. 'At the Hovel, I mean.'

'Hargrove?' said Cliff as he puffed on his pipe. 'Never really thought about him. Why?'

'It's just that...well he behaved rather oddly the other night. He told me he'd overheard our conversation about the diary, while we were in the hall.'

'Did he, by George? He seems far too well bred to be listening at key-holes.'

'I don't think he was deliberately listening,' said Clarice.

'Sound seems to travel a long way in that house. But I rather got the impression he wanted to have a look at the diary. He seemed quite disappointed I'd given it to the police.'

They walked into the shade of woodland, leaving the open ground behind them. Cliff tapped his pipe out on a tree stump.

'There's no mention of anyone with the initials J.H. in it,' he mused. 'Or anyone else that could be Hargrove, as far as I can recall. Why should he take an interest?'

'I don't know,' said Clarice thoughtfully. 'But there's something I don't like about him.'

'Seems a harmless enough sort to me, but if you're concerned, I'll keep an eye out.'

'Thanks, it's probably nothing,' said Clarice.

They walked in silence for a long time, passing the ridge of Hampstead Lane then down through steep wooded slopes until they passed North End Road.

There was something familiar about the little tree-lined streets around here, thought Clarice. What was it? Then she felt a stirring in the back of her mind.

'Wasn't this where that other girl was found?' she asked Cliff. 'The one you've been writing about?'

'What? Oh, yes – you mean June Philpott. She was found collapsed on Wildwood Road, which is just over there if I recall. I did a little digging around here when I first started my article. Marks of strangulation were found on her, but she had no recollection of how she got there.'

'How dreadful,' said Clarice. 'At least she survived.'

'Yes, she was fortunate,' said Cliff. 'According to her statement, she was walking on the Heath on her own and got lost. Night fell and the next thing she knew, someone attacked her from behind. She came to in some sort of shed or outbuilding and wandered out, then collapsed in the road, where a passing motorist found her. The police tried to trace her movements but she could only give a very vague description of where she'd been lying.'

'What on earth could have happened to her?'

'I think someone was intending to finish her off, but perhaps got disturbed and ran away.'

'It all sounds simply awful. What happened to her?'

'Moved away from the area, I think. I tried getting in touch for my article but there's no trace of her. Can't say I blame her. The police accused poor Stanley Franks for the attempt, but the prosecution collapsed.'

'You don't think he did it?'

'No. The motorist who found Miss Philpott said he saw someone lurking on the Heath nearby, and he picked out Franks from a police photograph – he was known to the police, you see, for petty offences. But at the last minute the defence produced two witnesses who saw Franks ten miles away at the time. It's my opinion he was "fitted up", as they say.'

'You mean the police knew he was innocent?'

'I didn't say that. I think they were desperate to find who did it, and Franks just happened to fit the bill. The poor blighter wasn't the full shilling and couldn't stand up for himself. He probably even started to believe he *did* do it.'

They reached North End Road and crossed into Golders Hill Park. 'I'm parched,' said Clarice. 'Shall we stop for tea somewhere?'

'There isn't anywhere round here,' said Cliff. 'Only the Bull and Bush, and they won't be open yet.'

'Oh,' said Clarice. 'I suppose we'd better be getting back then. Lunch will be fairly soon.'

'I say,' replied Cliff. 'If we walk all the way into Golders Green, we can get a cup of tea there, then take the tube back. My feet won't survive a walk all the way home.'

'Your feet, or your shoes?' asked Clarice with a grin.

'There are at least twenty years of wear left in this pair,' said Cliff, as he lifted a foot and peered at the large crack in the side of the upper.

They continued through the neat landscaping of Golders Hill Park and then past large detached villas, a red-brick nonconformist church and a cinema, and then the gleaming white war memorial marking the centre of Golders Green. They found a shadowy teashop inhabited by elderly ladies with lapdogs who stole glances at them and whispered to each other as they sat down.

'I don't suppose you serve beer?' asked Cliff loudly to the wizened waitress who arrived to take their order.

The elderly ladies whispered more intently, and Clarice stifled a grin.

'This is a temperance area, sir,' she sniffed. 'There are no licenced premises within a mile of here.'

'What an utterly absurd notion,' said Cliff. 'We might as well be in the United States of America. Oh well, tea it is then.'

'You don't suppose there's a connection, do you?' said Clarice as they sipped their tea. 'Between the attack on, what was her name, June Philpott, and Evelyn?'

'Possibly,' said Cliff thoughtfully. 'It's an angle I've been working on in my article. Both women were about the same age, height and build, with similar colour hair; both attacks took place in the same part of London, both were strangulation.'

At the mention of 'strangulation' a distinct hush fell upon the tea-room, and Clarice was relieved when Cliff asked for the bill. She attempted to 'go dutch' but he would not hear of it, and also paid her fare when they got on the tube.

As the train rocketed into the tunnel, Clarice felt a sense of horror and despair. This must have been where Evelyn was attacked, she realised. Then something light-coloured flashed past the carriage and was gone.

'What was that?' she asked Cliff, raising her voice over the noise of the train.

'I've noticed that before on this line,' said Cliff. 'I think it's some sort of passing loop set back from the rails.'

Clarice frowned, unsure of exactly what a 'passing loop' might be. As they handed over their tickets at Hampstead station, Clarice smiled at the ticket collector.

'Excuse me, but I noticed a sort of alcove or gap of some sort momentarily on the line between here and Golders Green. Please tell me I'm not seeing things.'

'You're not, miss,' said the collector with a chuckle. 'Seen you before, ain't I, but you're usually going the other way I think.'

'That's right,' said Clarice. 'I go from here to Camden Town'.

'Yes,' replied the man, 'so you wouldn't go the other way normally. That's not an alcove or a gap, that's Bull and Bush.'

'Bull and Bush? But isn't that a public house?'

'It is, miss, but it's also what we call a ghost station.'

'I don't understand.'

'When the line was built 20 odd years back,' continued the man, 'they built a station there. But they never finished it. There was supposed to be a housing estate built nearby on the Heath, but it got cancelled, and so there was no point opening the station.'

'How interesting,' replied Clarice. 'Did…'

There was the rattle of a lift door behind them and a stream of passengers emerged.

'I'd like to tell you more,' said the collector, 'but perhaps another time.'

'Yes of course,' said Clarice. 'You've been very helpful.'

Travers and Hollis sat in their makeshift office in Hampstead police station. Despite the fine weather there was a distinct air of gloom about the place. A look of disgust crossed Travers' face.

'Well, that's that then,' he said. 'Lerner's in the clear. Has he gone yet?'

'Duty sergeant's just released him,' replied Hollis with equal glumness. 'We couldn't hold him any longer.'

'He's a lucky man. Good work on finding that cabbie.'

'Thanks, sir,' replied Hollis. 'He saw Lerner come out of Golders Green station *and* pick up his car at Brent, so he can't have killed Miss Parks as he was a mile away from the scene at the time. What now, sir? Keep a tail on him?'

'No,' said Travers. 'We haven't got the men, and anyway, I think he didn't have anything to do with the killing. He's just the sort of fellow that leaves a nasty taste in one's mouth and I'd like to be able to get him for something.'

'You can't charge someone with playing away from home,' said Hollis.

Travers sighed. 'I know. I'm being sentimental again. Morality's for parsons to enforce, not policemen. Any luck with the usual suspects?'

'No,' sighed Hollis. 'Nothing. If the strangler was someone known, I think one of the narks would have come forward by now.'

'What about the stuff picked up from the tube carriage?' asked Travers. 'The fag ends, and so on. Any luck there?'

'Nothing remarkable,' said Hollis. 'And I should know, I

had to sift through most of the rotten stuff. There was an empty fag packet – French, that's a bit unusual – and a newspaper with a half-finished crossword puzzle, but not much else.'

A detective entered the room and placed a brown envelope on Travers' desk.

'Results in from the lab, sir,' he said.

'Thanks Collins,' said Travers. 'That'll be all.'

The man left the room and Travers eagerly opened the envelope.

'It's the results of the tests on the fibres found around Miss Parks' neck,' he said as he spread foolscap pages over the desk. He read out the contents of the file. '"Red, yellow and blue strands of a type of silk of Indian origin..." etcetera etcetera, "...containing traces of airborne pollen, most likely of the plant type..." can't pronounce that..."not being a plant native to the British Isles this suggests the article was worn for some considerable time in India or the near east rather than being imported directly into Britain."'

'Clever work,' said Hollis.

'Yes,' replied Travers. 'Looks like she was strangled with a scarf, or tie, perhaps, made in India, and worn by someone there for a while. And who do we know with connections to India?'

'Hargrove. But the married couple, ah, Mr and Mrs Stewart, they were out in India as well.'

'They've got an alibi, Hargrove hasn't, and there's a few things about him that are beginning to smell off. Oh, that reminds me - what did you find out at India House?'

'He's listed as a director of a couple of companies, like he said,' replied Hollis, consulting his notebook. 'Anglo-Indian Metals, and the Chandrapore Light Railway Company. So he was telling the truth.'

Travers rubbed his chin thoughtfully. 'His former landlady said he wore an Indian Army tie, so that's in keeping with the Indian companies. A railway company, you say?'

Hollis nodded. The mention of a railway rang a very small and distant bell in the back of Travers' mind. It was that feeling he had had before; there was some connection between the railway and Evelyn's death that he could not quite bring to light, no matter how hard he forced his brain to work. He quickly decided that forcing it would be of no use, and turned to Hollis to reply.

'He was telling the truth that someone called John Hargrove is listed as a company director. That's all we know. And the previous address he gave us, at North End Terrace, was genuine. Know where that is?'

'I'm not from this neck of the woods, sir.'

'Nor me, so I'll tell you. It's about fifty yards from where June Philpott was found half-strangled on Hampstead Heath earlier this year. And his landlady said he liked going out for long walks at odd hours.'

Travers stopped, then glared at Hollis. 'I've just remembered something. You applied for the Lodge, didn't you?'

'Sir?'

'What's the name of that place where the Freemasons get all their rig from? Shop near Covent Garden somewhere, with all sorts of ties and things in the window.'

'Oh, you mean Amis, Kenton and Ravenscourt. But I never joined the Lodge in the end, I...'

'Never mind,' said Travers, and picked up the telephone. He asked to be put through to the shop in question, and spoke a few words with an assistant. He put down the telephone and grinned.

'Miss Parks had red, yellow and blue silk strands found

on her neck, from a fabric probably made – and worn – in India. Guess what colour the Indian Army tie is.'

'Red, yellow and blue, by any chance?' asked Hollis with a smile.

'Correct,' said Travers. 'And Hargrove was seen wearing one.'

'Lots of ties with those colours, though, sir,' said Hollis.

'Yes, but this one was most likely made – and worn – in India. That narrows it down a bit.'

'Might not have been a tie though,' mused Hollis. 'Could have been a scarf, or a belt or something.'

The telephone trilled. Travers picked it up. He listened for a few moments then said 'send her up.'

The two detectives rose as Clarice entered the room.

'Miss Thompson,' said Travers warmly. 'What can we do for you?'

Hollis gave up his seat and Clarice sat down.

'I'm sorry to trouble you on a Saturday,' she said.

'No trouble, miss,' said Travers. 'We work all hours of the day and night. Although we do have something urgent to follow up, so I'd be grateful if you'd be brief.'

'Of course,' said Clarice. 'It's just that I found out something rather strange today and I thought I should tell you…it's probably nothing.'

'That's all right,' said Travers. The young woman had been clever to find that diary, even though the lead about Lerner had been a dead end, and he was interested to hear what else she might have found out.

'I'll be the judge of that,' he said. 'Do go on.'

'Well, I, that is we, Mr Thorley and myself, were walking on the Heath this morning, and then we took the tube back. From Golders Green. On the way I noticed a sort of alcove, or recess, flash past the train. I spoke to the ticket collector about it and he said there is a disused station there.'

'What!' exclaimed Travers, more violently than he had intended. Suddenly, a rush of thoughts were fighting for prominence in his mind; connections and circuits were being formed rapidly, like some mental telephone exchange. He realised now what he had seen coming through the tube tunnel, and why the old poster showing the line through Hampstead had been playing on his mind after they had picked up Lerner.

Clarice looked slightly alarmed, and continued apologetically. 'I wondered if it could have some bearing on the case. The papers said that the police had no idea how the killer got off the train, and I just wondered…'

'Why the devil wasn't I told about this before?' demanded Travers, glaring at Hollis. 'You interviewed the guard and the driver and so on, why didn't it come up?'

'Ah…' began Hollis.

'Never mind excuses,' snapped Travers. 'Got the telephone number of the supervisor at the depot? Welland, I think his name was.'

Hollis leafed through his notebook and read out a number.

'Pardon me a moment, Miss Thompson,' he said brusquely, and picked up the telephone.

'Give me Speedwell 1214,' he snapped.

There was a pause and then Travers spoke again.

'Mr Welland? This is Detective Inspector Travers. Is it correct that there's a station *between* Golders Green and Hampstead? I see. And may I ask why nobody saw fit to tell me this during…I see, disused and only used for storage. Do trains ever stop there? Very rarely…what about the night of the murder?'

Travers sighed and looked at the assembled company with exasperation, then returned his attention to the telephone. 'Where can I get hold of him? Well would you kindly fetch him?'

The Inspector drummed his fingers impatiently on the telephone receiver and looked at the assembled company.

'Bit of luck. The driver of the train's in the depot on his tea-break. He's fetching him. Hello...yes...a question if I may about the murder we're investigating. Did you stop the train between Golders Green and Hampstead? For a signal, you say? Well why the devil didn't you mention it when you were asked bef...I suggest you don't take that tone with me. All right, fair enough, mistakes happen. None taken.

'And the signal stopped you for how long? As quick as that? Very well. Now, listen to me. Was the second from last carriage of the train within reach of the disused station? It was. I see. Thank you. Goodb...no, that's all. Goodbye. No, wait, put Mr Welland on the line again, would you?'

'Mr Welland, this disused station, does it have a ventilation shaft leading up to ground level, behind, ah, North End Terrace? Yes. Is there any access between ground level and the station...a spiral staircase. I see. No, that's all for now, but I expect I shall need to speak to you about it again presently. Goodbye.'

Travers replaced the ear-piece of the telephone onto its receiver.

'Damned incompetence,' he hissed. 'I'm sorry, Miss Thompson,' he added. 'You were right to let me know.'

'Look here, sir,' said Hollis. 'I've checked my notes, and I asked the driver if anything out of the ordinary had happened between the stations. He said no. I'm guessing he didn't think there was anything unusual about stopping for a red light, so didn't bother mentioning it.'

'No, you're right, he said as much just now,' said Travers. 'Happens from time to time apparently, to regulate the flow of traffic on the line. It's my own fault for not going into it in more detail with Welland before.'

He was about to ask Hollis more questions, but remembered the presence of Miss Thompson. His composure now fully regained, he turned to her.

'I'm sorry about that, Miss Thompson,' he said brightly. 'You were right to come to us with what you'd seen. I think we may have found the way our murderer managed to disappear from the train.'

'You mean, he got out at the ghost station?' asked Clarice. 'But surely, the sliding doors wouldn't have opened?'

'Wouldn't need to,' said Hollis. 'He could have got out the end door and squeezed round, between the carriages. I know, I've done it myself and got the dry cleaning bill to prove it.'

Travers leaned forward and stabbed his finger onto the desk. 'The driver said the train was held at a red light for about thirty seconds. The rear two carriages, that's including the one Miss Parks' body was found in, would have been in line with the disused station. He could have strangled her, slipped off the train, and got out via the ventilation shaft behind North End Terrace. From there it would be a twenty minute walk home.'

'It seems fantastic,' said Clarice. 'Wouldn't the guard have seen him?'

'The guard wouldn't need to look out, because the doors weren't opening,' said Travers.

'It's the only explanation that makes any sense,' said Hollis. 'It wasn't possible for our man to hide on the train or get out anywhere else undetected.'

Travers was deep in thought, recalling his conversation with the landlady at North End Terrace. 'And Hargrove knew about the ventilation shaft because...' He stopped himself short.

Clarice inhaled sharply. 'Did you say Hargrove?' she asked.

Travers sighed, annoyed that he had been thinking aloud. 'It's just a theory we're working on, miss, he said. 'Nobody in particular is under suspicion.'

'It's just that...' began Clarice.

'Yes?' said Travers.

'It's just that Mr Hargrove acted rather strangely the other day. He sort of...waylaid me on the landing; I think he'd been waiting for me while I was in the bathroom. He said he'd overheard Cliff – Mr Thorley, I mean – and myself talking about finding Evelyn's diary. Then he told me I ought to speak to him first if I found out anything else about the case.'

'Oh *did* he indeed?' said Travers. He looked at his wrist-watch. 'Do all the residents take tea at your establishment?' he asked.

'Most do, at five o'clock,' said Clarice. 'I'm afraid it's not much though, and usually rather stewed.'

Travers chuckled. 'I'm not after refreshment, Miss Thompson. But I think it's time we had another talk with Mr Hargrove. Hollis, take Miss Thompson down to the car, I'll be with you in a moment.'

After they had left the room, Travers lifted the telephone receiver to make another call.

Chapter Nine

Some time later the police car arrived at the Lovell Villa Private Hotel. Clarice opened the front door with her latch-key and let the two detectives inside.

'Shall I fetch Mr Hargrove?' she asked as she hung her hat and coat up by the door.

'That won't be necessary,' said Travers quietly. 'His room's at the top, I think?'

'That's right,' said Clarice, replying in a quieter voice herself. 'At the back. The one at the front is Mr Thorley's.'

'Very well,' replied Travers. 'You go up to your room please, and stay inside.'

Once they had seen Clarice to her room, Travers and Hollis climbed the narrow stairs to the second floor and knocked on the door at the back of the house.

The door opened a crack and Hargrove looked out. 'Oh, it's you,' he said. 'What do you want?'

'A few words, sir,' said Travers. 'If we may come in.'

'It's not particularly convenient at the...'

'*If* you don't mind sir.'

Hargrove reluctantly opened the door and the two men stepped into the room. It was small and sparsely furnished, and seemed at odds with what Travers knew of Hargrove's character and background.

'What's this about?' asked Hargrove suspiciously.

'A few points to clear up,' said Travers, looking around

the room. There was a deep sense of gloom here, he thought, not helped by the peeling Victorian wallpaper, the dark furniture and the cracked washstand in the corner.

'Can you tell us again where you were on the night Miss Evelyn Parks was found strangled?'

'For the third, or is it the fourth, time, Inspector,' said Hargrove, 'I was in the Maybush public house in Hampstead. They had a lock-in, so there was late service and I decided to stay on. I was in the snug listening to the wireless, and I left just after 11 pm and came straight home.'

'So you say, sir. But the trouble is whilst the barmaid at the Maybush can remember you were there that night, she can't recall when you left.'

'I can't help that.'

'No sir. But there's a few other things I'd like to clear up. For instance, where did you live before you came here?'

'North End Terrace, if you really must know.'

'I meant before that.'

'Do I have to give you every blasted address I've lived in...'

'Kindly don't raise your voice, sir,' said Travers. 'We don't want to disturb the other residents, do we?' He crossed to the open door of a heavy dark wardrobe, where three ties hung on a hook. He fingered them idly.

'Got an Indian Army tie?' he asked.

Hargrove swallowed. 'No,' he said.

'That's odd,' said Travers. 'Because your former landlady at North End Terrace remembers you wearing one.'

'Why on earth were you talking to...I...that is to say, I did have an Indian Army tie, but I don't have one now. I lost it.'

'Pity. But you oughtn't to have worn one anyway, really.'

'What the devil do you mean by that?'

'I put through a telephone call to the War Office before we came here. Like us policemen, they work all hours, so it didn't matter that it was Saturday half-day. I asked them to check if there was any record of anyone in the Indian Army in the last 30 years called John Hargrove. Turns out there wasn't. Handy things, these card indexes they use. So why did you wear that tie?'

'I'm not answering any more damned fool questions,' snapped Hargrove. 'Now, will you leave?'

He stepped to the door, which was blocked by Hollis.

'I'm sorry sir, but we can't do that,' said Travers. 'I'm afraid you'll have to come with us.'

'For what possible reason?' said Hargrove.

'Because,' said Travers slowly, 'we found evidence to suggest Miss Evelyn Parks was strangled with an Indian Army tie.'

Such evidence, thought Travers, was not conclusive, but mentioning it was worth a try, he decided. The ruse appeared to work.

The colour had drained from Hargrove's face. 'All right,' he sighed. 'Would you allow me to put my mackintosh on? It's hanging on the door.'

'One moment sir. Give it to him, Hollis,' said Travers.

The sergeant took the coat down, and held it out by the arms like a valet, continuing to block the door as he did so.

'Thank you,' said Hargrove, and shrugged the coat on. Then with one fluid movement, he twisted Hollis' arm and hurled the man off-balance. He fell heavily against the wardrobe, and Hargrove disappeared through the bedroom door.

With a curse, Travers launched himself at the exit, but it

was now blocked by Hollis' legs as he slumped forward, and a heap of clothes which had fallen from the wardrobe.

A quick glance showed him the man was not badly hurt. He managed to get the door open and squeezed himself on to the landing, hearing the thunder of rapid footsteps on the stairs and then a crash as the front door slammed shut.

Travers followed as fast as he dared on the dimly lit staircase with its slippery drugget, and emerged into the front garden. Hollis, now recovered and following closely behind, almost crashed into him as he suddenly stopped on the garden path.

'Barnes,' he yelled, as he fumbled in his pocket for his whistle. He was about to blow it then saw the officer in question picking himself up from the pavement in front of the garden gate.

'Tried to stop him but he laid me out, the swine…' he said groggily, rubbing his jaw.

Travers ran briefly up and down the street while Hollis helped Barnes to his feet, but it was hopeless; Hargrove had disappeared into the dusk.

From her room, Clarice heard the sound of heavy footfalls on the stairs, then the slamming of the front door. She listened for a few moments, then emerged on to the landing, to see Mrs Sibley looking up from the hall.

'What on earth is going on?' she called out. 'Has someone fallen downstairs?

'I don't think so,' called Clarice. Then she gasped in surprise as a figure emerged from the shadows of the stairway to the second floor. It was Mr Stewart, followed by his wife.

'Are you all right, Miss Thompson?' he enquired. 'Only we heard sounds of a struggle upstairs.'

'Quite all right, thank you,' said Clarice. She began to have an idea of what might have happened, and walked tentatively towards the staircase.

'Shall I go up?' offered Mr Stewart.

'Oh yes, do,' said his wife. 'There might be someone lying dead up there.'

Clarice felt a twinge of distaste at Mrs Stewart's dramatising attitude, and proceeded up the stairs herself.

'I'm sure it's nothing to worry about,' she said. If truth be told, she wondered whether something had happened between Hargrove and the detectives, and she felt instinctively that the presence of the Stewarts would only confuse matters.

She reached the top of the stairs and looked across the landing to where the door of Hargrove's room stood open. She saw an overturned chair and a wardrobe at a dangerous angle with a jumble of clothes spilling out.

She jumped in fright as a figure emerged from the room on her left.

'What the devil's going on?'

'Oh, it's you Cliff,' said Clarice with relief. 'Did you hear anything?'

'I'd dozed off,' replied Cliff, rubbing his eyes. 'Must have been all that fresh air on the Heath. Heard all sorts of pounding on the stairs. What happened?'

The front door bell clanged and there came the sound of male voices from below; a brief protest from Mrs Sibley, then the sound of a man speaking on the telephone in the hall.

'It's the police, my dear,' called Mrs Stewart from downstairs. 'It seems Mr Hargrove has assaulted a constable, and run off. How simply awful.'

'Come along, Mary,' said her husband. 'Let's get out of their way and allow them to do their job. If we're lucky we may still get a cup of tea downstairs.'

A few moments later, Travers and Hollis arrived at the top of the stairs.

'Go back to your rooms, please,' said Travers, brushing past Clarice and Cliff on the landing.

'Look here, what's going on?' demanded Cliff.

'We're very busy, Mr Thorley…' began Travers.

'Dash it all, we've a right to know what's going on in our house under our noses. Is Hargrove a suspect?'

Hollis stepped forward aggressively but Travers put out a restraining arm.

'It's all right,' said the Inspector. 'Search the room, Hollis. I suppose you do have a point, sir. And I believe you're connected with the newspapers?'

'Well, I…'

'Can you get something in the papers tomorrow?'

Cliff looked at his watch and frowned.

'I can if I telephone it through.'

'Good. If the sub-proofreaders or whoever you speak to give you any trouble about accepting it, mention my name.'

Cliff hurled open the door of his room and sat down at a battered desk. There was a mechanical screech as he quickly rolled a sheet of foolscap into his typewriter.

'Fire away.'

Travers began dictating rapidly and Cliff's long fingers flew over the typewriter keys.

'"Police are urgently seeking the whereabouts of a man suspected of involvement in the recent murder of a young woman, Evelyn Parks, on a tube train at Hampstead, Thursday week last. Name John Hargrove, of Lovell Gardens NW3, previously of North End Terrace, also NW3;

age around 40, height, approximately five feet nine inches, medium to heavy build, clean shaven, dark hair. Last seen wearing a grey lounge suit, dark tie and fawn coloured mackintosh, no hat. This man is considered dangerous and should not be approached by the public." Got that?'

Cliff rammed the carriage return home and looked over the sheet of paper. Clarice couldn't help being impressed at how quickly and accurately he typed – somehow she had thought of him as a 'hunt and peck' typist, and she felt a twinge of jealousy.

'Think so,' replied Cliff. 'But what about fleshing it out a bit? The human interest angle. For instance…'

'Don't talk soft,' said Travers. 'Get that printed, and *only* that.'

'Come and have a look at this sir,' interrupted Hollis from the doorway.

'Get on the telephone to your newspaper chums,' said Travers to Cliff, as he left the room and crossed the landing.

'I've found these, sir,' said Hollis, holding out some documents. 'Passport and some other papers. But they're not in the name of John Hargrove.'

Travers examined the passport. 'It's him all right. But this is in the name of Wilby. Colonel Eric James Arthur Wilby, trade or profession, army officer…place of birth, Bombay…well I'm damned.'

He turned to see Cliff and Clarice watching him with interest.

'Look, do you mind, you two? This is police business.'

Cliff waved the typewritten sheet of foolscap. 'Now come along, Inspector. Fair's fair. It'll take you an age to get through to the newspapers now and who knows what sort of rot they might publish if you rely on some muck-raker you don't know to write it for you? At least let us watch you in action as the consummate professionals I am sure you are. After all, what if the good sergeant finds another clue before I despatch my epistle to the press?'

'You talk too much,' said Travers. 'All right, amend the statement to include Hargrove's real name, Wilby, and hurry up about it.'

Cliff returned to his typewriter and Clarice remained on the landing, uncertain whether to stay or go. She watched as Hollis stepped back into Hargrove's room.

'There's something else, sir,' he said. 'Looks like it fell out of the wardrobe when he pushed me into it.' He gingerly lifted the item off the heap of clothing using the end of a pencil. It was an Indian Army tie.

'Well, well,' said Travers. 'Looks like his landlady at North End Terrace was right. What about the other bits and pieces?'

Hollis looked at the papers he had taken from the drawer. As he read, his eyes widened. 'Couple of news cuttings…*Times of India*…Englishwoman found strangled in Bombay…Jean Wilby, wife of…Colonel Eric Wilby.'

The next day was Sunday, and the usual calm and quiet (some might call it tedious) atmosphere of the Sabbath at the Lovell Villa Private Hotel was disturbed by the events of the previous night.

The residents had performed their usual observances. Thorley had dozed in bed; Miss Grant and Clarice had attended matins at nearby St John's, and the Stewarts, favouring the plainer devotions of the Scots, had been to the Presbyterian church on Finchley Road.

Mrs Sibley, though professing to be a Christian of the

devoutest type, was always quick to point out that she 'didn't have time for church' as there was 'far too much to do for luncheon'. That meal was now over, and the residents dawdled over coffee in the lounge while Mrs Sibley and Vera fussed over the cups and saucers. A pile of newspapers had been brought in by Cliff, and he now eagerly scanned the pages.

'Here's another,' he said proudly. 'I say, they even included my name in this one,' he said, stabbing his finger at the paper. 'By Clifford Thorley, special correspondent.'

'I don't see what's so special,' said Mrs Sibley. 'You only took down what that policeman told you, and telephoned it through to the papers. Anyone could have done that.'

'Well I think you did a splendid job, young man,' said Miss Grant, sipping at her coffee like some tiny humming bird taking nectar from a flower. 'If it helps to apprehend that awful man, it will have been worth it.'

'I'm just glad you kept the name of this establishment out of it,' said Mrs Sibley. 'It's bad enough having a guest get murdered, without it turning out to be another guest that done, I mean, did it.'

Clarice frowned. 'We don't know that Mr Hargrove – or Colonel Wilby – the police found out his real name in his passport, you see – we can't be *sure* he did anything. The police don't seem entirely convinced he's the murderer.'

'Ye-es,' said Cliff doubtfully, 'but they found some news cuttings in his room last night that suggested he might have killed his wife in India. Ever hear of that case while you were out there, Stewart?'

'Can't say I did,' said Mr Stewart. 'India's a big place, mind you. What were the details of the case?'

'Travers wouldn't let me look at the cuttings, of course,' replied Cliff, 'but first thing tomorrow I'm going to the newspaper archive library to look the case up.'

'Oh, that settles it, he must be the strangler,' said Mrs Stewart, who seemed distinctly nervous. 'Why else would he go running off like that? And he knocked down a policeman, they say.'

'*And* damaged my furniture,' added Mrs Sibley. 'I shall have to speak to the police about compensation, when they catch that so-called Mr Hargrove. It'll cost at least ten shillings to put that right, and if they hang him I dare say I shan't see a penny of it. '

'I do not think we shall see him again,' said Miss Grant. 'I expect he has gone abroad. Probably to Calais, on the channel packet steamer. I believe that is what criminals "on the run" usually do. Or am I thinking of duellists? At any rate, we can sleep soundly in our beds, I think.'

'I wouldn't be so sure,' said Mr Stewart. 'If he left his passport here, as Miss Thompson says, he might find it difficult to get away. And the ports are bound to be watched. It's my opinion he'll have gone to ground, as they say.'

'Well whatever he does, that's the last we've seen of him, I hope,' sniffed Mrs Sibley. 'I shall certainly be more careful of references in future.'

'Now don't go blaming yourself, Mrs S,' said Mr Stewart. 'You can't be expected to know the fellow would turn out to be a murderer.'

'That's very kind of you to say so, Mr Stewart, I'm sure,' said Mrs Sibley. 'Well, you two have had a lucky escape, in that case,' she added, nodding at Clarice and Vera.

'We?' asked Clarice. 'In what way?'

'What I mean to say is,' said the landlady, 'the papers are saying they think the strangler who killed poor Miss Parks is the same as left that girl for dead on Hampstead Heath a few months ago. They were both said to be aged around 20, slimly built and with fair hair and complexion.

That's you and Vera to a "t", that is. You might have been Mr Hargrove's next victims, if the police hadn't scared him off.'

There was a crash as Vera dropped one of the cups she had been stacking.

'Oh you haven't broken it?' chided Mrs Sibley.

'You don't mean some strangler's coming after me just because of the colour of my 'air?' gasped Vera.

'Let's not get too carried away,' said Cliff. 'Admittedly there was a physical similarity between the victims, but a lot of girls in London answer that description. I shouldn't worry yourself, Vera. Anyway, Hargrove's gone now.'

It was good of him, thought Clarice, to calm the poor girl's nerves like that. But she couldn't help thinking back to when Hargrove had emerged from the shadows under the stairs, and there had been that strange light in his eyes. Perhaps it *had* been a lucky escape.

There was no Sabbath calm for Inspector Travers and his men. Alerts had been sent out to railway terminuses, ports and even Croydon Aerodrome in the hope of finding Hargrove, aka Wilby. Cliff's item in the newspapers had begun to attract interest, and Travers had had to bring in another detective on his day off solely to deal with telephone calls to Scotland Yard.

He and Sergeant Hollis now stood in a muddy alleyway behind North End Terrace outside the brick-built ventilation shaft leading to the abandoned station below.

'I must say I think it a bit much for me to be dragged out here on a Sunday,' said Mr Welland, the supervisor from Golders Green depot. 'I was just sitting down to my dinner when you telephoned.'

Travers sighed. 'I daresay your wife can warm it up in the oven when you get back. I won't keep you long.'

'It never tastes the same that way,' muttered Welland, as he looked through a large bunch of keys. 'Ah,' he said, producing one of them. 'This is it. We don't normally use this entrance. If I remember the duty rosters correctly, nobody has been here for almost a year.'

'What exactly is the station used for?' asked Travers.

'Purely for the storage of materials required for track maintenance,' said the supervisor. 'The main lift shafts were never sunk, owing to the cancellation of the plans to build a housing estate nearby. The railway company then decided the station would not have enough traffic to justify such expense.'

'I see,' said Travers. 'Let's have a look then.'

Welland stepped forward to insert a key into the large brass padlock on the door, but Travers stopped him.

'I'll do that if I may,' he said, taking the key in one hand and wrapping his handkerchief around the other. 'We may need this to be dusted for prints. Hello....'

He wiggled the top of the padlock and it swivelled open. 'Well I'll be...' he said. 'The bally thing's open.'

'This is most irregular,' said Welland. 'One of the maintenance staff must have left it unlocked. I shall have words.'

'It was put back in place though, to look as if it was locked,' said Hollis. 'That wasn't an accident.'

Travers pushed the heavy wooden door open, and lit his battery torch. A blast of warm air, heavy with the smell of damp, wafted up to greet him. Ahead was a small vestibule with a flight of metal spiral steps leading downwards.

'Look over here, sir,' said Hollis, shining his own torch

on a corner of the vestibule. 'Signs that someone's been lying down there, I'd say.'

Travers looked over. 'Yes, the dust has been disturbed, it seems, though I'd say some time ago.'

'Didn't the Philpott girl say she thought she'd been kept in a shed or an outhouse of some sort?' said Hollis.

'You're right,' said Travers thoughtfully. 'But then why wasn't this place found when the police searched the area?'

'Lots of sheds and garages and things between here and, where she was found on the Heath,' said Hollis. 'Could have been any of them. There's no mention of this place in the reports, I know that because I've gone through them.'

'Yes, I'm not too happy about the way that case was conducted,' said Travers. 'Ransome – the man in charge – retired soon after under a bit of a cloud. I think that's why the Hampstead CID called us in when Miss Parks was found. They didn't want another botched job.'

'Is there anything else you wanted to see, gentlemen?' asked Welland impatiently.

'Does that staircase lead all the way down to the platform?' asked Travers, shining his torch towards it.

'Yes,' said Welland. 'It's a while since I've been here, but I recall it's a long way down.'

'Right, lead on then,' said Travers.

'Is this really necessary?' asked Welland. 'It's an awful long climb back up...'

'The exercise will do you good,' said Travers impatiently. 'Go on.'

The three men walked down the narrow curving staircase for what seemed to Travers like hours, but was probably less than five minutes. The air became warmer and the noise of trains louder; eventually they reached a dimly lit, dusty platform, piled high with cables, insulators and other electrical equipment that Travers could not identify. The station's name, 'North End', was written out with dark-coloured tiles along the grimy wall.

'I thought this place was called Bull and Bush,' said Travers.

'That's just because it's near the pub of the same name,' replied Welland. 'It's "North End" officially.'

'Bit of a waste, if you ask me,' said Hollis. 'All this built for nothing.'

'You might be surprised at the number of similar stations on London's underground railways,' said Welland. 'I believe there are several. Now, have you seen all you require?'

'Some footprints here, sir,' said Hollis, shining his torch on the dusty platform. Travers added the beam of his own torch to the spot, and then moved it along the platform edge. 'Quite a few of them. Different sorts – heavy boots mostly. I'm guessing that's maintenance men?'

'There have been works along the line recently,' said Welland, 'and as you can see some items are stored here.'

Travers heard a humming sound from the track and a distant rumbling. He looked up, but before he could step back, there was a roar of noise and a flash of light as a train thundered past him, just inches away from his nose.

He jumped back, yelling an oath, and collided with a stack of insulators, almost falling over in the process.

'God almighty,' he said angrily after the train had left. 'There's no warning.'

'Why would there be?' chuckled Welland. 'Nobody comes down here except people who know what they're doing, and we railway men always know when a train's coming. You get a sixth sense for it.'

Travers sighed. 'Well why didn't you tell...oh, never mind. I think we've seen enough down here. I need some fresh air.'

Some ten minutes later they arrived, breathless, into the open air. Welland locked the padlock properly this time, and with a warning that he might be required to open it again soon, hurried off to salvage what he could of his Sunday dinner.

Travers and Hollis walked slowly to the car, parked at the end of North End Terrace.

'It's beginning to make sense, Hollis,' said Travers. 'What if it happened like this. Hargrove liked long walks on the Heath, his landlady said. He also knew about the ventilation shaft. He grabbed June Philpott one night and throttled her until she passed out. But he didn't want to finish her off there and then. Probably wanted to take his time over it.'

'Savour the moment, you mean?' said Hollis.

'Perhaps. Who knows what goes on in the mind of someone like that? He got her to the ventilation shaft, and either picked the lock, or it wasn't locked in the first place, and shoved her in there. She somehow managed to get away, though according to her statement she had no memory of it. The police are all over the area for weeks afterwards, probably knocking on doors and so on, so he decides to move away from North End Terrace to Lovell Gardens. There, Miss Parks catches his eye. Similar looking girl to Miss Philpott.

'He follows her about a bit – we know someone did, from the entries in her diary – and one night can't control himself any longer and strangles her on the train. Then, he can't believe his luck when the train stops at the ghost station, because he knows that means he can get off the train without being seen.'

'Could be,' said Hollis. 'Bit of a risk though. What if someone had locked the door at the top?'

'He could have broken out eventually,' said Travers. 'He'd still be safer there than staying on the train. It's possible he deliberately left the padlock unlocked after Miss Philpott got away, in case he wanted to use the place again.'

'He'd have to be quick though,' said Hollis. '*If* he strangled Evelyn, that would be just before 11pm. He'd have to be back at the Maybush long before 11.45 because that's when the barmaid said the last customers left. I suppose he could do it if he hurried.'

'Yes, you might be right,' mused Travers. 'Easy enough if he caught a 'bus. I don't like this uncertain barmaid though. The Maybush was having a lock-in, so she'd have to let him in especially. Surely she'd remember unbolting the front door for him?'

'Not if he let himself in the back way,' said Hollis. 'I had a look round there. There's the usual ablutions round the back in a yard, with a low wall. Anyone could get over that. They wouldn't lock the back door because people would be going in and out for the necessary.'

'Well spotted,' said Travers, as they reached the police car. 'I think we're on to something. Then there's this business with his wife in India. I read the cuttings. She was strangled, and a young Indian was charged but they couldn't prove murder so he got life for manslaughter instead.'

'You think it was Hargrove all along, sir?' said Hollis.

'We've associated him with three stranglings, two of them fatal, and we've found a tie in his room with fibres that may match those found on Miss Parks' neck. It's not looking good for him, is it? By the way, get that tie over to the lab as soon as possible for a comparison, will you?'

'Already done it, sir.'

'Good man. Get in the car then.'

'Are we off home? At least Welland's got a warmed up dinner in the oven to look forward to. Mine will most likely be in the dustbin if I stop out any longer.'

'Don't talk daft. You're going to the War Office. I daresay there will be someone on duty. Find out everything you can about Hargrove stroke Wilby's record. I'm going to the India Office to look into his wife's case. I'm pretty sure they can send messages by telegraph to India in a few seconds these days.'

'Phew, bet that costs a pretty penny,' said Hollis, as he sat down on the back seat of the car.

'Can't think of a better use of taxpayers' money,' said Travers. 'Let's get moving. When, and I stress when, not if, Hargrove gets picked up, I want to already know everything there is to know about him.'

In her little half-basement bedroom at the side of the Lovell Villa Private Hotel, Vera Beech pulled the bedcovers over herself and waited until the bed began to warm up. She had been saving up for an india-rubber hot water bottle, but never seemed to quite have enough money for one because she had to send back most of her wages to her parents in Balham.

She was not particularly keen on her Sunday half-holiday; it seemed to be over so soon that it was almost not worth bothering about. She rarely had any free time on that day anyway, as most of it was spent at the evening service of an obscure sect that met in a little chapel in Child's Hill. Her parents knew the minister, and insisted on regular attendance lest she fall into the 'worldly ways' of London.

There wasn't much chance of that, she thought glumly. She knew she wasn't particularly pretty, though she also knew if she had the money she could make herself look nice with the right clothes and makeup. But that wouldn't go down well at the chapel, she realised.

There had been a man there – Walter – about her own age, not what she would call handsome, but he had ever such a nice speaking voice when he read the lesson, and he was doing well in a local paint merchants. She had been surprised and flattered when he had invited her for tea at a Lyon's on two occasions, but she began to feel she wasn't worthy of him.

He had talked with alarming intensity about things she didn't really understand, such as 'the gifts of the Spirit', 'the priesthood of all believers' and 'the heresy of Trinitarianism'. So she just let him talk, and he didn't seem to mind.

Then one Sunday he didn't appear at chapel, and she received a long rambling letter from him stating that he had had doubts about *'sola scriptura'*, whatever *that* meant, and had gone over to the Roman Catholics to become a priest! Well that, of course, was that, because she knew they weren't allowed to marry.

She switched off the light and closed her eyes. She wondered where Walter was now. In a monastery somewhere, she supposed. She realised she had forgotten to say her prayers, and began to do so, but drifted off to sleep before she could finish.

She was awoken some time later by a scratching sound. It was not unknown for mice – sometimes even rats – to be heard in her room, so she thought little of it. Then, she thought of Mr Hargrove and realised he was still at large. Her heart began to kick violently in her chest and she opened her eyes and reached out to switch on the light.

In the same instant that it was turned on, the light was extinguished by a heavy blow. A shadow fell over her, and the last thing she felt was a searing pain in her throat as strong hands pressed her neck into the pillow.

Chapter Ten

The following morning the slumbering residents of the Lovell Villa Private Hotel were woken by a piercing scream from the basement.

Clarice was first to reach Mrs Sibley, who emerged from Vera's room with her hand clutched to her mouth.

'Oh it's too horrible,' she cried.

Clarice hurried into the room but the moment she saw Vera she knew nothing could be done for her; she lay completely still, her eyes staring glassily upwards, with a bluish tinge around her lips. A man's tie lay around her neck. It was dreadfully cold in the room, and the thin curtains wafted in the chilly breeze coming through the open sash window.

'We musn't touch anything,' said Clarice firmly. 'Mrs Sibley, would you telephone for the police please? Mrs Sibley!'

The woman was on the verge of hysterics so Clarice moved her bodily to the stairs and escorted her up them. By now Cliff, Miss Grant and the Stewarts, in various states of undress, had appeared from their rooms.

'What's happened,' asked Miss Grant querulously. 'Is it a fire?'

'It's Vera,' said Clarice. There was no way of putting it gently. 'She's been strangled. Mrs Sibley is going to telephone for the police. I think we should all wait in the sitting room, together, until they arrive.'

'Oughtn't we to dress first?' asked Miss Grant. 'I have no wish to meet the police in my night attire.'

'It looks as if the killer got in through a window downstairs,' said Clarice quickly. 'That means he may still be in the house. We shall be safer if we stay together.'

'You're right of course,' said Cliff. 'Clarice, take the other ladies into the sitting room and barricade the door. Stewart and I will search the house.' He took a walking stick from the stand by the front door and brandished it. 'Come along, Stewart.'

'Well...I...' began Stewart doubtfully, but his wife interrupted.

'Mr Thorley is right,' said his wife. 'You need to make a thorough search. And Mr Thorley, make sure you stay with my husband. If there *is* a killer here he could pick you both off individually. Oh, this terrible house! I don't want to stay here a moment longer!'

Mrs Sibley had by now summoned the police by telephone, and Clarice herded her, Miss Grant and Mrs Stewart into the sitting room.

Ten minutes later the two men returned. 'Nothing,' said Cliff. 'Whoever did it probably got out the window, the same way he came in. If...'

He was interrupted by the clanging of the doorbell and Clarice looked out of the bay window to see two uniformed policemen at the door.

'Barnes deserves a medal,' said Travers, as he and Hollis made their way down the back stairs to the basement of the Lovell Villa Private Hotel. 'I make that just 25 minutes from the Yard to here. And in the morning rush, too.'

Hollis, who was unshaven, unbreakfasted and distinctly unhappy at being roused so early on a Monday morning, merely grunted his assent.

Despite having seen many murder victims Travers could not help a brief flash of revulsion cross his face when he surveyed the maid's bedroom.

'Have you touched anything, Mrs Sibley?' asked the Inspector.

The landlady, standing outside the threshold, merely shook her head; Clarice, who along with Mrs Sibley had been asked to accompany the detectives, answered for her.

'I told her not to,' said Clarice.

'Good,' said Travers.

'Was the door locked when you found her, Mrs Sibley?' asked Travers.

Mrs Sibley swallowed hard. 'Yes. She wasn't up to make the breakfast, and there was no reply when I knocked, so I used my spare key. Did I do wrong?'

'No, that's all right,' said Travers. 'Would you wait outside with Miss Thompson, please? I'll want to speak to you again in a few minutes. Oh, and would you be so kind as to tell the other residents to stay in the house? They can wash and dress now if they like.'

Once the two ladies had left, Hollis looked around the room while Travers examined the body.

'Jemmy marks on the window ledge, sir,' said Hollis. 'And the gravel outside's been disturbed.'

'Same marks on the throat as with Miss Parks,' said Travers. 'Only this time he's left the murder weapon.'

He carefully lifted the tie, which was distorted from the force exerted on it, and looked underneath.

'There's some writing on the label in china pencil,' he said. 'Well well. John Hargrove.'

'He's a cool one,' said Hollis. 'I thought he'd be halfway to South America by now, instead of coming back here.'

'So did I,' said Travers thoughtfully. 'That's why I didn't bother putting a man on watch outside. Perhaps I should have done.'

'Nobody in his right mind would come back here once he'd got away,' said Hollis. 'We must be dealing with a lunatic. And besides, we don't have a man to spare.'

'Don't you think it's a bit odd a man using a false name writes that name on his tie?' asked Travers.

'Well if he was going under a false name he wouldn't put his real name on it, would he, sir? He probably took it to the cleaners and they wrote on it, they do that sometimes.'

'Hmm, perhaps,' replied Travers. 'All right, seal this room off. Have a look outside and then speak to the doctor…ah, talk of the devil, he's here.'

The police doctor nodded solemnly to the two men and began his examination.

'Death by strangulation,' he said. 'Sometime between one and two a.m., I'd say. Can't say much more than that now.'

'Thank you,' said Travers. 'Right, let's get a move on. I'll speak to the other residents. And when we're done here I'll telephone to the commissioner. We need to double the number of men on this case.'

With a weary sense of familiarity Travers entered the sitting room and began interviewing each of the residents in turn.

Mrs Sibley merely repeated what she had said already; that she had entered Vera's room, seen her lying dead on the bed and had run out screaming.

Cliff, hurriedly dressed and looking distinctively scarecrow-like, piqued the Inspector's interest when he asked him what he had been doing the night before.

'I was up late,' he said, 'and went out for a walk. I can't provide an alibi, if that's what you're...'

'No, sir,' interrupted Travers. 'We're fairly certain Hargrove's the man we want. 'What time were you out?'

'About half past three,' said Thorley. 'I just wandered the streets for a while.'

'Doesn't Mrs Sibley keep the door locked at night?' asked Travers.

'She only bolts it from inside. There's nothing to stop anyone going out and coming back in, assuming nobody bolts it again while one's out.'

'I see, sir,' said Travers. 'When did you come back?'

'About four. But there's a rather odd thing that only makes sense to me now.'

'What's that?'

'Well, I was walking up the road to Heath Street, and, of course, hardly anybody's around at that time. But I saw a chap going in the direction of the house on the other side of the road, and it could well have been Hargrove.'

'You weren't sure?'

'I only glimpsed him for a second or two under a streetlamp, then he disappeared. My goodness, if I were sure it was him, I would have apprehended him, or at least raised a hue and cry. But the idea of Hargrove coming back here seemed fantastical, and I must have just put it out of my mind.'

'I see,' said Travers. 'That's all for now. We're going to have to move quickly on this before Hargrove strikes again. Would you show Mr Stewart in?

After speaking to Mr Stewart and his wife individually, Travers learned their normal routine had not been disturbed; they had listened to the wireless in their room and then gone to bed; Mr Stewart thought he *might* have heard a window opening in the early hours, but was not sure; Mrs Stewart added nothing of interest and spent most of the interview announcing that she could could not pass another moment in such a house.

Miss Grant, whose nerves were worsening, said she had taken a sleeping draught and was dead to the world (she apologised for the expression) by nine p.m.

It was Clarice, however, who had the most useful piece of information for Travers.

'I did think I heard a sash opening,' she said, as she perched on the arm of the Chesterfield sofa.

A woman police constable had been summoned to the house, and had busied herself with making cups of tea in the kitchen; Mrs Sibley was in too much of a state of nervous exhaustion to cope with the task. Clarice sipped from her cup, and Travers, suddenly ravenously hungry, drank his in one go and lit a cigarette as a makeshift breakfast.

'What time was this?' he asked.

'About one o'clock. I looked at my alarm clock because at first I thought I'd slept through the night and it was time to get up. The mornings are quite dark at this time of year.'

'I see. Then you went back to sleep?'

'Not immediately. I was in that rather odd state when one's not quite sure if one's awake or asleep.'

'I know what you mean. Go on.'

'Well, shortly after I heard the window sash, it can't have been more than two or three minutes later, I heard a sort of crunching sound which faded away. My window was slightly open, you see, as I like fresh air when I'm sleeping. I assume the sound was footsteps on the gravel path that runs by the side of the house.'

'But you didn't hear that before you heard the sash window open?'

'No...I say, perhaps what I heard wasn't footsteps on the gravel, but someone landing on it after jumping out of the window. I obviously wouldn't have heard that before someone climbed in through the window, would I?'

Travers could not help being impressed by the calmness and clear thinking of this young woman, and suddenly wished he were ten or fifteen years younger. As was his habit whenever a sentimental thought crept into his mind, he shook it off quickly.

'And then you heard footsteps on the gravel?' he asked.

'I think so, but only briefly. I then went back to sleep, as I honestly wasn't sure if I were awake or dreaming. Oh, I might have heard someone coming through the front door later, I've no idea when, and anyway I couldn't swear to it. Now I wish I'd done something about it. Poor Vera.'

'Don't blame yourself, Miss Thompson. There was nothing you could have done. If the police doctor is correct, Miss Beech was already dead by the time you heard those footsteps. Now, I'd better let you get to your classes. I'll be passing through Camden Town shortly if you'd like a lift.'

'That's very kind of you,' said Clarice, 'but I shall telephone to say I'm not coming today. I rather think I – and Cliff – Mr Thorley, I mean, ought to stay here with Mrs Sibley and Miss Grant. The Stewarts have each other but those two don't have anybody. I shan't go to the college until tomorrow.'

Travers smiled, which for him was a rarity. 'That's very civil of you, miss,' he said. Then he paused, unsure of how how to broach a difficult subject.

'Ah...I don't wish to alarm you, Miss Thompson,' he said slowly, 'but I suggest you don't go anywhere alone at present.'

'Why ever not?'

'We're doubling our efforts to catch Wilby – or Hargrove,

as he's known, but he's clearly a highly dangerous and cunning man. We never expected him to come back here, but he did, and that's on my conscience. I'll be putting a guard on the house from now on, so you'll be perfectly safe here, but I can't vouch for your safety outdoors.'

'But why should I be particularly at risk?' Clarice asked, then her face fell. 'Oh...I see what you mean. Evelyn, Vera, and that other woman, the one in the papers, June something...'

'June Philpott.'

'Yes, of course. They were all about the same age, similar hair and figure and that sort of thing. And I suppose I'm much the same as that.'

'The thought had occurred to me,' said Travers, 'but I didn't want to alarm you. But we think now Hargrove may have killed his wife in India, and the newspaper photos show she was a similar looking woman. It's possible Hargrove's got a particular type of girl in mind when he strikes.'

'How dreadful...well, I shall be careful of course, but I shan't cower away at home for the rest of my life.'

'That's the spirit, Miss Thompson, but I'm not asking you to stay here any longer than is absolutely necessary.'

'Very well. May I go now? I haven't had a chance to tidy myself up.'

'Yes of course,' said Travers, standing up. He was tempted to tell her that she looked perfectly all right as she was, but he thought better of it.

'Would you show my sergeant in, please?' he said instead.

Travers realised things were about to move very quickly, so he spoke rapidly to Hollis.

'Find anything outside?'

'Not much, sir. The gravel's loose and you can't make

out footprints in it. No prints in the garden either. Fingerprint chaps are dusting the window frame now, but looks as if he had gloves on. Anything turn up with the residents?'

'Couple of things. Thorley was out walking in the early hours – seems he's a bit of an insomniac – and thinks he might have seen Hargrove.'

'That makes sense,' said Hollis. 'And the other thing?'

'Miss Thompson thinks she heard a sash window opening downstairs at about one a.m, and then footsteps on the gravel path. Later, she thinks someone might have come through the front door, but that was most likely Thorley when he came back from his moonlit stroll.'

'I've got reservations about that Thorley,' said Hollis. 'I still think he might be tied up in this. What if it was him came through that window and he made up a story about seeing Hargrove to throw us off the scent?'

'I did think of that,' said Travers, lighting another cigarette, and checking his notebook to prompt his memory. 'But his alibi's sound for the first murder. And why would he say he saw Hargrove about four a.m. going *towards* the house? If he wanted to pin the murder on him, he would say he'd seen him at one a.m. or thereabouts, coming away from the place.'

'Suppose so,' said Hollis rubbing his chin. 'Hargrove's linked with those other cases too, the June Philpott strangling and his wife in India. By the way, sir, have you heard anything from the India Office about that yet?'

'No,' said Travers curtly. 'They seemed to think looking up records on a Sunday was some sort of social faux-pas and got very shirty when I told them to get their superior in off the golf course. I'll try them again today. How did you get on at the War Office?'

'Not much,' said Hollis. 'He had compassionate leave

round about the time his wife was killed, and then he went on half-pay and moved to England. Effectively retired, though he's still on the reserves list. His home address is some place in India with a bally silly name I can't pronounce, but his London place is the Naval and Military Club. I had a look at his room there but it was empty.'

'Good work anyway,' said Travers. 'We'll keep a watch on it.'

He heard raised voices outside the house and looked through the bay window to see a police constable jostling with a group of men in mackintoshes brandishing notebooks and cameras.

'That's all we need, the press,' said Travers. 'Get rid of them, Hollis…no, on second thoughts, send them away nicely. Brief statement, tell them there's been another murder and it's imperative we find Hargrove as soon as possible etcetera etcetera. I want that man's photograph on every front page and I want him found. He's running rings around us.'

'He's leading us a merry dance, all right sir,' said Hollis as he went to the door. 'I'll see if we can get a bulletin on the wireless as well.'

'What did you say?' asked Travers. Something had stirred in the back of his mind prompted by what Hollis had said, but the man had already left the room.

The fog returned shortly after mid-day; Hampstead took on the appearance of a high peak cloaked in clouds. But rather than fresh mountain vapour, these clouds were thick, cloying and yellow; the city was now in the grip of what was known as a 'real pea-souper.'

Clarice sat in her room alone. Mrs Sibley served a sparse sandwich luncheon for the remaining residents. Cliff had gone to one of the large libraries to find out all he could on the murder of Hargrove/Wilby's wife, in the hopes of getting another article into the newspapers. Mr Stewart had announced he was going to work, leaving his wife to fret in her room alone.

After some discussion of whether mourning should be worn for the death of a servant, Mrs Sibley and Miss Grant left to travel to Balham by underground railway in order to console Vera's parents. It seemed, from what Clarice could work out, that although Vera was not Mrs Sibley's natural daughter as she had rather romantically suspected, she was at least some sort of relation – a third cousin twice removed or something along those lines.

'Almost family in fact, well, in law, anyway,' Mrs Sibley had said as she buttoned up her black fur overcoat. 'So I feel it's the least I can do.' Miss Grant had murmured sympathy and looked admiringly at herself in the large mirror in the hallway, adjusting the new black hat she had worn for Evelyn's funeral. It seemed that mourning for a servant was acceptable after all, and they hurried off to the tube to get to Balham 'before any dreadful reporters arrived.'

Clarice lit her little bed-side lamp; it was now almost dark outside despite not being much later than one p.m. A deep despondency settled on her and she could not help thinking over the events of the last few days in intimate detail.

She was sure now she had heard the sash window downstairs opening in the night, but also that the sound of the front door opening had been much later; in fact she recalled now the grey pre-dawn light just beginning to appear behind the curtains, which would fit with Cliff coming home about four a.m.

But there was something about the footfalls she had heard on the gravel which was not right. There had been the sound of someone jumping on to the gravel, presumably from the window ledge after strangling poor Vera, then a couple of footsteps, then nothing.

She crossed to the window and lifted the sash, recoiling slightly as the acrid fog hit her throat. Fortunately visibility was still around thirty feet or so, and she craned her head round to look at the gravel path at the side of the house.

Yes, she thought; it was just as she had remembered it. A thick, deep gravel path which ran alongside the house and then widened across the front garden. She remembered vaguely Mrs Sibley saying it was a deterrent to burglars because anyone walking up, or down, that path from the street would make an awful noise. Her room and Vera's were the only ones with windows on that side.

Had the killer gone into the back garden, instead? Surely not, as it was surrounded by a high wall with a gate that was kept padlocked. No, he must have gone through the front garden. Unless...

She hurried downstairs and opened the front door; as she did so, the policeman at the front gate turned to look at her and she smiled apologetically.

'Just getting a breath of fresh air,' she said, and the man nodded in response.

She walked past the large bay windows round to the side of the house. There was a border, or flowerbed, which ran along the front of the house. The only way anybody could leave Vera's room by the window and get away without more than two or three strides across the noisy gravel would be if he walked on that flowerbed.

She looked closely at it for the signs of footprints, but

there were none. Of course, the police would have checked for such things, but the soil was hard and dry and she could make out no trace of human activity. And if he did cross that border, it meant the only other place he could go without making any noise on the gravel – was into the house.

Had Hargrove let himself back in and somehow hid in the house while the police had been all over it? It was too fantastical!

There was something else, too, nagging at the back of her mind, as she let herself back into the house. She looked at the hall table, which was today devoid of letters, and suddenly remembered what it was. When she had passed the letter to Mrs Stewart, she had noticed the previous address struck through – North End Terrace, NW3. But that was where Inspector Travers had said *Hargrove* had lived.

She went into the sitting room and found the previous day's newspapers which, in the absence of Vera, had not yet been used for their normal function of lining the dustbin. She hurriedly looked through them to find Cliff's article and yes, there it was – North End Terrace.

She fetched the little London street map that was kept by the telephone directory in the hall. She checked the index and found North End Terrace. It was a little road that cannot have had more than a dozen houses in it. Then she saw the name of another road nearby whose name she also recognised. Wildwood Road. She looked through the newspaper article; that was the road in which June Philpott had been found half-strangled. Clarice was sure that the Stewarts had never mentioned this. She then recalled Mrs Stewart had seemed anxious to intercept the letter before anyone else saw it. It was all extremely odd.

She pondered on this for some time. All the evidence

pointed to Colonel Wilby – or Mr Hargrove, as she still thought of him, but he had never struck her as a murderer. Rather troubled in some way, perhaps, but not violent. But then again, she realised she'd never met any murderers before, at least not knowingly, so was in no position to judge.

Her musing was disturbed by the telephone bell, which made her jump, and she crossed the hall and picked up the receiver. After stating the exchange and number, she heard an excited voice on the end of the line. It was Cliff.

She listened for a while as he hurriedly spoke, and then replied in astonishment.

'It's just me here, yes, although I think Mrs Stewart is in her room. No, I think her husband's at work. Yes, there is a policeman outside. Lock myself in my room? Whatever for? Oh…really? But why would…Yes, all right, I'll wait.'

She replaced the telephone receiver and climbed the stairs. As she passed the Stewarts' room, she heard sounds of rapid movement from within, as if drawers were being flung open and wardrobe doors slammed shut.

She hesitated, and a feeling of tightness rose in her chest. She hurried past the door and into her room, closing the door behind her, but she paused and listened; the bangings intensified and then there was a loud thudding sound. She decided she could not cower away any longer – what if Mrs Stewart, alone in her room, were in danger?

She took a deep breath and stepped outside on to the landing, to see Mrs Stewart hurling a large suitcase onto another already on the landing; that must have been the thudding noise she had heard.

'Oh Mrs Stewart, you're safe,' she exclaimed.

The woman looked up, an expression of fear and anger softening to a polite smile as she straightened up.

'Why on earth shouldn't I be, my dear?' she said. 'Just

doing a little, ah, spring cleaning.'

Clarice saw into the room beyond her; drawers had been left open, and various items of clothing were scattered on the floor; a large steamer trunk stood open on the threadbare Turkish carpet in the middle of the room. It did not look like any cleaning was being done, and it was certainly not spring.

'Mrs Stewart,' said Clarice cautiously, 'are you all right? You don't look quite well. Can't Mr Stewart help you, or is he still at work?'

'He...he's not here,' said Mrs Stewart hurriedly. 'Go back to your room, dear, just in case.'

'Just in case what, Mrs Stewart?'

'*Please* do as I say,' replied Mrs Stewart in a lowered voice, 'and lock the door.'

'Whatever for?' asked Clarice. 'If you're worried about Mr Hargrove coming back, there's a policeman at the front gate and we've only to call...'

She stopped, and suddenly realised why Cliff had told her on the telephone to lock herself in her room. For a moment she considered running to do so, but a sharp sense of indignation overcame her.

'Mrs Stewart, I don't think you are spring cleaning. I think you're leaving, aren't you? Leaving your husband.'

'What on earth do you mean?' said Mrs Stewart quickly. 'Go to your room for God's sake, like I said, and leave me alone,' she said as she hurled items of clothing into the trunk. 'I can't stay in this house a moment longer, I can't, I simply can't!'

Clarice realised the woman was becoming hysterical but she was determined to help her. 'If you really are leaving your husband, you'll need help with your things. I shall telephone for a taxi.'

'Oh you stupid girl,' said Mrs Stewart. 'Don't get

yourself mixed up in other people's business.'

Clarice took a deep breath. 'Mrs Stewart, are you leaving your husband because you think he was involved in Evelyn's murder?'

Mrs Stewart looked as if she had been slapped in the face. 'What…what on earth are you talking about?'

'Your last address,' said Clarice, 'that was on that letter you seemed very keen to take off me, was North End Terrace. That also happens to be where Mr Hargrove, also known as Colonel Wilby, lived, until about the same time you two came here. And also very close to where June Philpott was found half-strangled. And yet neither you or your husband mentioned that.'

'Why would we?' said Mrs Stewart. 'Mr Hargrove never told us where he used to live.'

'Perhaps he didn't, but we all talked about the article in the newspaper yesterday which said quite clearly that he had lived in North End Terrace. And yet neither you nor your husband mentioned it.'

'What's that got to do with anything?' snapped Mrs Stewart. 'Why should we mention having lived there? We don't talk about our past all the time.'

'But you do, Mrs Stewart. You and your husband are always reminiscing. About India, for example. Where, incidentally, your husband was named in connection with the murder of Jean Wilby – the wife of the man we know as Mr Hargrove.'

'How…how did you find out…?' Mrs Stewart asked weakly as she stepped back from the landing into her room.

'Mr Thorley found articles in the newspaper library,' said Clarice. 'He telephoned to tell me just now and is on his way back. And there's something else that's occurred to me just now. The police said they found the Indian

Army tie that they think was used to strangle Evelyn in Mr Hargrove's room. They said it was on top of a pile of his clothes that had fallen out of his dresser during a struggle. But I walked past that room while the police were out in the street looking for Mr Hargrove. The door was open and I glanced in. There *wasn't* a tie there, just a heap of white shirts. Which means someone in this house must have put it there.'

'I don't know what you're talking about,' said Mrs Stewart weakly. 'I'm leaving and that's that.'

'I don't think you ought to leave just yet,' said Clarice firmly. 'I'm going to telephone to Inspector Travers and ask him to speak to your husband when he comes home. Or perhaps it would be better to have the police meet him at his office. So if you are afraid of what he might do, there isn't any need.'

'I...don't you come in here...' said Mrs Stewart weakly, staring past Clarice into middle distance.

'Very well,' said Clarice. 'In fact I think I shall also speak to the constable at the gate, and...I say, are you sure you're quite well?'

Clarice stepped forward into the bedroom; she noticed the colour had drained from Mrs Stewart's face and she stared into space, appearing to be on the point of fainting.

'No...no,' she gasped. 'Not another one. Not her!'

Clarice realised that the woman was not staring into space. She was looking at something beyond Clarice's shoulder, but before she could turn, Clarice felt her head jerk back and a searing pain cut into her windpipe. Mrs Stewart hurled herself face down on the bed and wept; the room swam before her eyes, and then all was dark.

Chapter Eleven

Inspector Travers returned to his office in Scotland Yard in a bouyant mood, having met with the Commisioner and gained a few extra men in the hunt for Hargrove. All the major London terminuses were now being watched, as well as the continental ports and Croydon aerodrome. He was confident that the man couldn't stay hidden for long.

A detective entered the room and placed a buff manila file on Travers' desk.

'Ah,' said Travers, passing the file to Hollis. 'Some bedtime reading for you.'

'How's that sir?' replied the detective from his desk.

'Copies of the transcripts of all trials for capital crimes in India are kept in India House in London,' explained Travers. 'Including the trial for the murder of Wilby's wife. I want to see just what his involvement was. Have a look through, will you, and note down any mention of him.'

Hollis sighed, took the file and began skimming through it. An hour passed, and Travers tried to busy himself with paperwork on another case, but felt his mind wandering.

'Sir, there's something you should have a look at here,' said Hollis, leafing hurriedly through the court transcript.

'Not now,' said Travers impatiently. Something was nagging at him inside his head but it refused to come into focus, as if he were attempting to adjust a pair of faulty binoculars.

He lit a cigarette, in the hope it might encourage his thought processes. It worked.

'The tie,' he said, to nobody in particular.

'What's that, sir?' asked Hollis from his desk.

'Eh? Oh, just thinking out loud,' said Travers. 'There's something odd about the tie we found on Vera's body.'

'The name written on it, you mean?' asked Hollis. 'I know, it's a bit too neat, but it could be intended that way. Hargrove's a confident beggar, and it could be a sort of taunt. A calling card, you know. He's making it obvious he's done it and there's nothing we can do about it. But there's something you should look at here, sir…'

'It's not the name on the tie,' exclaimed Travers suddenly. He clicked his fingers and stood up.

'That tie was hanging in Hargrove's wardrobe when we spoke to him,' he said rapidly, beginning to pace up and down the room. 'I'm certain of it now, because I looked at three ties on the wardrobe door, in case one of them was Indian Army. Light green with a yellow check, that was it. I knew I'd seen it somewhere before. Hargrove was wearing a *plain* tie, dark coloured, when he gave us the slip. It can't have been used by him to kill Vera because he didn't have it when he left!'

'He could have gone up to his room and fetched it before he strangled her, though, sir,' replied Hollis. 'But as I was saying, you need to look at…'

'Why would he do that?' interrupted Travers. 'Why risk going upstairs to fetch a tie – with his own name written on it, mark you – when he was wearing one already that would do the job just as well? No, no, I think somebody else took that tie after we left, and that means someone else is involved…'

'That's just what I'm trying to talk to you about, sir,' said Hollis quickly. 'The court transcripts of the Jean Wilby murder case in Bombay. Her body was found by someone called Alec Stewart of the Imperial Tea Company.'

'Well I'll be...' began Travers slowly, and then spoke rapidly again. 'Stewart never mentioned that. I mean, when I interviewed him, you'd think he would have said he'd been a witness in another murder case.'

'Unless he had something to hide,' offered Hollis.

'But why didn't he know who Hargrove really was?' asked Travers.

'Something about that here,' said Hollis, pointing at the transcript. Wilby – that's Hargrove – was called as a witness but was unable to attend the trial, being on active service with his regiment at the time. Maybe Stewart never met Wilby, and he wouldn't recognise his name because he changed it to Hargrove.'

'This is all very strange,' said Travers, with a sharp exhalation. 'And there's something else. Something you said about Hargrove leading us a merry dance. Wait a minute. I should have checked this before but it went clean out of my mind.'

He flicked rapidly through his notebook, then picked up the telephone.

'Get me the BBC, right away,' he snapped.

Fifteen minutes later he replaced the receiver and turned to Hollis. 'I knew something was up when you talked about putting out a bulletin on the wireless and Hargrove leading us a merry dance. Hargrove said he was listening to a political talk on the wireless in the pub on the night of the murder. But Stewart said he and his wife were listening to a dance band programme.'

'Could have been on one of those foreign stations,' offered Hollis doubtfully.

'No, Stewart definitely said it was the national programme,' said Travers, looking at his notebook. 'But according to the BBC, there *wasn't* any dance band music on the national programme that night. There usually is around that time on Thursdays but on the night in question, it was cancelled in favour of a special broadcast on the economy.'

'So Hargrove was telling the truth, but Stewart wasn't?' asked Hollis. 'But his wife backs his story up, that's why we didn't consider him as a suspect.'

'And we were bally silly not to,' said Travers angrily. 'For all we know she's covering for him. There's another thing, now I think of it,' he added. 'Where's all the litter picked up from the tube train? The fag packets, and so on?'

'All in there,' said Hollis, pointing to a large cardboard box. 'Just on its way to the evidence room.'

Travers rummaged through it and finally produced a folded copy of the *Times*. He flicked through the pages and stopped.

'Here it is,' he said. 'I remembered there was a discarded paper. It's from the day of the murder. Look, it's got one of those new word puzzles. Cross-words, they call them. Now Stewart said on the night of the murder he listened to the dance band on the wireless and he did a cross-word puzzle. His wife said he's always doing them. Fetch me that tie, would you? The green and yellow one, I mean, that was found on the maid's body.'

'You're in luck, sir,' said Hollis, as he produced the article from a brown envelope. 'This one's due to be analysed in the lab.'

Travers laid the tie carefully alongside the newspaper and pointed with a pencil to the label and the puzzle. 'I'm no expert but wouldn't you say the block letters spelling out 'John Hargrove' on the tie are the same handwriting as the ones written on that puzzle?'

'Certainly similar, sir,' said Hollis, 'but even if it's

written by the same person, it doesn't prove…'

'Yes, yes,' said Travers impatiently, 'but it all starts to smell off, doesn't it? The maid gets strangled with a tie that couldn't have been used by Hargrove, but had to have been taken by someone else in the house. Of the other people in the house, Stewart's the only one who's lied to us about his alibi.'

'We don't know he lied, sir,' said Hollis. 'He might have got mixed up…'

'Mixed up, and also forgot to mention he'd previously appeared as a witness in a strangling murder case? And lives just downstairs from Hargrove's room, which wasn't kept locked, enabling him to pinch that tie?'

'I suppose it's a bit odd,' said Hollis, 'but is that enough for us to go on?'

'It's enough for me to want to have a very long chat with Mr and Mrs Stewart individually, and preferably in a police cell,' said Travers. 'Unless Wilby is found soon, we've got nothing else to go on and I'm prepared to clutch at straws at this point. Get your hat and tell Barnes to be round the front quick-smart.'

'Up to Hampstead, then?' asked Hollis.

'We'll pick up Stewart first, from his office,' said Travers, 'then get his wife at home later.'

'I'll be glad when this is all over,' sighed Hollis, 'and we don't have to drive half-way across London just to ask someone a few questions.'

A few minutes later, Travers and Hollis were standing in front of the personnel officer of the Imperial Tea Company, Mincing Lane.

'As I said,' began the heavily bespectacled functionary, 'Mr Stewart telephoned to say he was ill and that he would not come into the office today. Is it an urgent matter?'

'A routine enquiry, sir, that's all,' said Travers.

'Will you wish to visit him at home?'

'Yes, we will, sir.'

'I take it you have his address?'

'Yes sir, Lovell Gardens. We'll be on our way.'

He turned to go but the personnel officer called out. 'I don't think that is correct, Inspector,' he said with a frown. 'I seem to recall…one moment, please.'

Travers watched with interest as the man took out a file from a cabinet and opened it on the desk.

'Oh dear, my mistake,' said the man. 'You are indeed correct. I see now that he has moved. To Lovell Gardens, as you said. I had in my mind his previous address, North End Terrace, NW3 '

Travers and Hollis exchanged a sudden meaningful glance, and hurried out of the office.

Cliff frowned as he stepped out of the telephone box outside the Central Newspaper Library in the Charing Cross Road. He hoped he hadn't frightened Clarice by telling her to lock herself in her room, but he had felt suddenly afraid for her safety.

It had been quite a surprise finding Stewart's name mentioned in the *Times of India* press reports of the murder of Jean Wilby. It seems he had known her as a fellow worshipper at the Scots church in Bombay, and come across her body by chance one night in a park. He claimed to have seen a group of young Indians running away; one of them had later been found guilty of manslaughter and sentenced to life imprisonment, as murder could not be proven.

But it was all very strange, he reflected. Why on earth

hadn't Stewart or his wife mentioned any of this? They were always going on about their time in India and how much better things were out there than in London. And more suspiciously, why didn't they know who Wilby, alias Hargrove, was? *Did* they know who he was, but for some reason pretended not to?

He looked at his watch; it was nearly four. Stewart would be back from work in a couple of hours and he wanted to make sure he was there to meet him and ask him some questions. Ought he to telephone the police, he wondered? No, he decided. He was only just on their good side now and he didn't want to risk them thinking him a meddling fool again.

He turned up his jacket collar and shivered, as the damp fog thickened around him, and hurried to the nearest underground station.

Why was her bed so cold and hard? That was Clarice's first thought as she began to regain consciousness. She tried to pull the blankets tighter, but realised her hands were bound, and there were no blankets. She was not in bed, but lying on a concrete floor in a small space lit only by the dim light from a grimy window.

She tried to call out, but pain seared through her throat and she realised she was gagged. Panic began to rise up within her but she forced herself to stay calm; she was still alive and that meant she still had a chance. She breathed slowly and deeply and looked around her as best she could.

She saw the dim outline of the Lovell Villa Private Hotel through the window, and after a few moments she recognised where she was; it was the small garage at the side of the house, in which Mr Stewart kept his motor car, and Cliff kept his motor-cycle. Yes; there it was to her left; the dark, oily-smelling shape of the car, looking enormous from such a low angle. She froze; she was not alone.

At the front of the car, she saw a pair of men's shoes, and the cuffs of his trousers. She could not see any more as the man was bending down, the rest of his body concealed by the car's nearside mudguard.

There was a grunting noise from the man, and then a mechanical clicking sound. It came again, and Clarice realised that whoever it was was attempting to start the motor car with a starting handle.

Then she heard another sound from behind her and swivelled her neck painfully round to see a man emerging from a hiding place behind Cliff's motor-cycle. Her eyes widened as she realised it was Hargrove.

He moved towards her in a low crouch, looked at her and then put his finger to his lips, nodding his head towards the front of the car in an exaggerated manner.

Clarice lost all her carefully gained sense of control, and screamed from behind the gag. Only a weak whimper emerged, but it was loud enough to alert the man bending down at the front of the car. He stood up quickly, and she saw that it was Alec Stewart.

Before he could react, Hargrove was upon him, launching his right fist at the man's face. But Stewart was quick, ducking sufficiently to receive only a harmless glancing blow, and his own right hand shot back in return. Unlike Hargrove, Stewart had the advantage of holding a heavy metal starting handle, and the relatively light blow he struck with it on Hargrove's cheek was sufficient to knock the man down instantly.

Hargrove slumped over the car bonnet, blood trickling

from the side of his face, and Stewart pushed him off to the floor as if he were nothing more than a sack of potatoes. He swiftly bound and gagged the man with some torn rags from a shelf, then opened the rear passenger door of the car and moved towards Clarice.

She closed her eyes, knowing she must try to appear unconscious. An attempt to escape now would be impossible, but if he was going to take her somewhere in the car, she might just have a chance.

She felt her body stiffen involuntarily with disgust as Stewart's fat fingers touched her neck, but were then withdrawn; he was perhaps feeling for a pulse. He grunted and then lifted her into the rear seatwell of the car. Some sort of musty blanket was placed on top of her, and the door was closed.

Then she heard the mechanical clicking again, and this time the engine roared into life and the car began to move. There was a brief pause as, presumably, Stewart got out of the car to close the garage doors. He got back into the car but then stopped it again. Then she heard voices.

'Just a moment, please.' A man's voice, authoritative. Clarice's heart leapt as she realised it must be the policeman on watch at the gate.

'Oh, it's you, constable,' said Stewart. 'Gave me a bit of a shock coming out of the fog like that. Can't see more than five yards in this.'

'You're a resident, here, sir?'

'That's right. Alec Stewart's the name, I live here with my wife.'

'I see. What's the registration number of your vehicle, please?'

'Why on earth do you...oh yes of course, I see. Can't be too careful, can you? I could be anyone. It's LA 415. Would you like to see my driving licence?'

'That won't be necessary sir. Carry on.'

Clarice tried to scream, but even without a gag it would have been useless. Her throat was so painful that only a whisper came out. Instead, she used all her strength to raise her bound ankles up and then kick as hard as she could on the inside of the rear door, hoping that she could force it open.

'Just a moment,' said the policeman. 'What's that noise?'

Stewart revved the engine. 'Bit of engine knock I think. She's like that after a cold start.'

'No, this was from the back.'

'Ah, that's the exhaust then. She'll be all right after a quick tap with this. Could you shine your torch round the back, constable?'

'Happy to oblige sir. Here, there's someone…'

The constable did not finish his sentence. Instead, there was a sickening thud similar to that which Clarice had heard when Hargrove had been hit with the starting handle.

Cliff emerged out of Hampstead tube station into a silent world that appeared to be entirely muffled in dirty cotton wool. He crossed Heath Street cautiously, jumping to one side as an unlit van passed dangerously close in the gloom. He then hurried down Lovell Gardens. As he approached the house he heard the revving of an engine and a little Austin shot past him, nearly knocking him off his feet.

'Hi, damned fool!' he shouted angrily. When he reached the Lovell Villa Private Hotel he noted with annoyance that the garage doors had been left open, exposing his motorcycle to the elements. Had that been Stewart that had nearly run him down? He was the only other resident who used the garage. He entered the little building quickly and nearly tripped over the prone body of Hargrove.

'What in God's name...?' began Cliff, then he bent down and pulled the gag from Hargrove's mouth.

'What's going on?' he demanded. 'You're wanted for murder.'

Hargrove's eyes slowly opened and he spoke in a faltering voice. 'It's Stewart you want, not me. He's got Clarice. I'm...there's no time to explain. Get the policeman from the front.'

'Where the devil's Stewart taking Clarice?' said Cliff. 'If you know, you'd better tell me, or so help me I'll...'

'I want to get him as much as you do...' groaned Hargrove. 'Go after him you fool. I think I know where he's taking her. Telephone the...'

'Where, blast it?' said Cliff frantically, shaking the man by his shoulders.

'Back of North End Terrace...' said Hargrove feebly. 'He's used it before...steps down to...' Then he passed out.

Cliff made a split second decision. There was no time to lose. He mounted his motorcycle at the rear of the garage, and attempted to kick-start it. Nothing happened.

'Start, you damned heap of junk!' he exclaimed. As if in affronted response to his words, the engine sparked into life with an angry growl. Cliff bumped his way out of the garage, turned swiftly, and within seconds was careering up Lovell Gardens towards Heath Street. He suddenly remembered he ought to have told the policeman where he was going, and about Hargrove in the garage, but there was no time now, he thought, as he gunned the engine.

It was only when he turned into Frognal Lane that reason took over and he realised what a foolhardy undertaking he was involved in. He wore no coat and his ungloved hands were already beginning to suffer from the cold, damp air that was moving rapidly over them. The front lamp of the motorcycle did little to pierce the thick fog. He knew the route to North End Terrace roughly, but in this blasted fog would he ever be able to find it?

At least, he thought, Stewart can't drive too fast either. To do so would be foolhardy and attract unwanted attention. At Heath Street there was a traffic block and his heart leapt as he recognised Stewart's car inching slowly forwards, the way ahead blocked by a lorry. He had him now!

Before he could reach the car, the lorry suddenly moved and Stewart turned left. A traffic policeman then stepped out in front of Cliff, holding up some sort of flare, his white-gauntleted hands barely visible in the fog. Cliff knew if he stopped, he would lose the car, and so swerved around the policeman, causing him to jump aside and drop the flare in a sputtering heap on the ground.

Cliff careered round the corner after the car, feeling the front wheel mount the greasy pavement and he gasped as he passed within inches of a perambulator pushed by a nanny in a Norland uniform. The woman screamed and pulled its occupant to safety.

'Terribly sorry,' shouted Cliff over the roar of the engine, as his left foot scrabbled for purchase on the pedal, and he was off again. The sharp sound of a police whistle was just audible and he groaned inwardly, then realised that was a good thing; with any luck the alarm would now be raised and he would soon gain a police escort.

Emboldened by this thought he let out the throttle as far as it would go and the motorcycle shot up Heath Street, gaining ground against the little car which struggled on the steep incline. 'Blasted idiot!' shouted Cliff, as he narrowly missed a horse and cart which plodded out of a side street. The carter, straining violently at the reins, shouted something far less polite in reply.

The traffic thinned out at Whitestone Pond but the fog became thicker, swirling and rolling off the Heath in damp, dripping clouds, so wet that it seemed hardly possible they could remain in the form of vapour. Cliff could no longer feel his hands and he struggled with the motorcycle's controls, particularly the footbrake, as he thundered down the steep hill of North End Road.

His machine had no speedometer but he estimated they must be doing almost fifty miles per hour. So much for his idea that Stewart would keep his speed down. It was all he could do to keep the motorcycle stable and his eyes on the little red light ahead of him. Suddenly, the light disappeared and he realised the car must have turned right into a side road.

Then the motorcycle lurched; the engine coughed twice and then cut out, and Cliff was forced to slither to a humiliating stop on a pile of damp leaves, only just managing to remain upright. He had run out of petrol.

'Come on Barnes,' said Travers to his driver as the police car crawled its way through the north London traffic. 'We could have walked faster than this.'

Finally they arrived at the Lovell Villa Private Hotel and Travers frowned as they pulled into the drive. Something was not right.

'Where's the man on point duty?' he asked Hollis.

'Should be out the front,' said the sergeant. 'Probably inside telephoning in for his hourly report, or checking the back.'

'The garage doors are open,' said Travers.

The two men turned their mackintosh collars up tight against the damp fog, and made their way along the gravel path.

'Ring the bell, Hollis,' said Travers, pointing to the large old-fashioned bell pull by the door.

A distant jangling sounded deep within the house but nobody came to the door. Travers rapped with the knocker several times with the same result. Eventually he stooped down and was about to shout through the letterbox when he heard the sound of a woman sobbing from the landing.

'Someone in trouble, I think,' he said. 'Get this door open.'

Hollis removed his hat and deftly used it to protect his fist as he punched a hole in one of the stained-glass panes in the door, then he reached through to open the latch.

They found Mrs Stewart lying on the rug in her room, with two large bruises on her face. She was semi-conscious and crying bitterly.

'Mrs Stewart, can you talk to us, please?' said Travers firmly but gently.

'Too late...,' she murmured between sobs.

'What's too late?' demanded Travers.

'I tried to stop him, but he bashed me…'

'Who did? Was it your husband? Are you saying your husband attacked you?'

'I said no more...not again...but he wouldn't listen...have to get away from him...'

'Mrs Stewart, where is your husband now, please?'

The woman stared into space, as if she could not see the two detectives in front of her, and laughed bitterly. Travers noticed the woman's Welsh accent had become more pronounced.

'Thought I'd stay quiet, he did...that I wouldn't tell.

He's got his little secret, I've got mine. Well I don't care anymore, see. I don't care who knows it.'

'Hollis,' said Travers, 'see if there's anybody else in the house and if you can find any brandy, bring it here. Then telephone to Hampstead police and get a doctor and a woman constable over quick smart.'

Hollis nodded and left the room.

'Now, Mrs Stewart,' continued Travers, 'please answer my questions as best you can. Where is your husband?'

The woman stared into space again. 'He thought I'd stay quiet because without him I'd be nothing. He was right, you know. I *was* nothing. Came from the gutter, from a Bombay slum. But he picked me out of it and that was our little secret…'

Travers raised his eyebrows in surprise and finally Mrs Stewart focused her gaze on him instead of the middle distance.

'That's right, Inspector. I'm not what you think I am. My mother was Kashmiri, pale skinned she was, and my father, well, nobody knows who he was but he was white enough to let *me* pass for English. All I needed to do was get the accent right. Then nobody could find out, see?

'You don't know what it's like,' she continued. '"Chi-chi", they call us out there. "Lick of the tarbrush" when they're being less polite. If the *pukka-sahibs* knew, I'd be back in the slums. Alec knew but he kept it quiet…and the price was letting him get away with his…habits. When we left India I thought he'd stopped, but then it started again…'

The woman collapsed again and this time Travers was unable to rouse her. He considered slapping her face, but before he could do so, a shout came from downstairs.

'Sir,' yelled Hollis. 'Come down here, quick.'

There was the sound of a scuffle and a crash as a large

item of furniture was overturned. Travers hurried downstairs to the hall to see Hollis, Barnes and another uniformed police constable struggling with a fourth man. It was Hargrove.

Within a few seconds Travers had handcuffed him and sat him down at the foot of the stairs.

'You've got to listen to me,' gasped Hargrove. 'Stewart knocked me out. He's taken…'

'Quiet, you,' said Travers, then turned to the police constable, who had a large bloodstain on the side of his head. 'You all right?'

'I'll live, thank you, sir.'

'You're already in deep trouble, Hargrove, or should I say Wilby,' said Travers. 'We can add assaulting a police constable to the other charges.'

'*I* didn't do that you damned fool,' gasped Hargrove. 'I found him in the bushes by the garage. Stewart must have clobbered him as well. He's…'

'Shut up and let him talk,' barked Travers.

'He's right sir,' said the policeman, rubbing the angry looking bruise on the side of his ear. 'It was some Scotch fellow in the motor car, he got me with a spanner or something. Looked like he had someone tied up in the back of his car. I managed to crawl into the bushes but must have passed out. I only just came round when this gentleman found me and when I recognised who he was from the mug shots, I attempted to arrest him. I hope I did right sir, I…'

'Wait, wait,' said Travers. 'You mean Alec Stewart's gone off in his car, with someone tied up, after knocking out two men? Why the devil did he…'

'Because he's got Clarice Thompson,' interrupted Hargrove. 'That's what I was trying to say. Have you got a car?'

'Yes, yes,' said Travers, a cold creeping sense of horror rising up inside him. 'Where's he taking her?'

'Get these blasted handcuffs off and I'll come along and show you,' said Hargrove. 'But for the Lord's sake be quick about it.'

'You're going nowhere,' said Travers decisively.

'This one's out for the count, sir,' said Hollis, looking at the policeman who had now slumped on to the overturned hall table.

'Concussion, probably,' said Travers. His mind was racing and he rapidly considered what was the best use of his remaining manpower.

'Hollis, cuff Hargrove to the stairs and keep an eye on this fellow passed out here. Barnes, there's a woman in the first floor front. Don't under any circumstances allow her to leave. Oh, and give me your car keys.'

Barnes nodded and handed over the keys. 'Where are you going sir?'

'I've an idea where Stewart's headed. Hollis, telephone to Hampstead again and tell them to get everyone they've got over to the old tube station entrance behind North End Terrace. That's right, eh, Hargrove?'

Hargrove nodded sullenly.

'And get through to that supervisor at the depot, ah, Welland,' continued Travers rapidly, 'and tell him to stop the trains on either side of Bull and Bush station. Threaten him with obstruction if he gives you any trouble.'

'But sir,' protested Barnes, 'you can cut that fog with a knife and fork. It'll take an hour to drive there.'

Travers did not reply; instead he hurried down the garden path to the police car.

Chapter Twelve

By the time Stewart's car slowed down, Clarice was already exhausted from trying to release herself from the tight rags which bound her hands and legs. She had tried to kick the door again when the car had slowed down earlier, hoping there was a policeman controlling the traffic, but to no avail; the rolling motion of the vehicle had somehow pushed her too far away for her legs to reach.

She decided instead to try to release the bindings holding her hands together. The knot felt as if it were large and clumsy. She felt her fingers gain purchase on it and loosen it a little, but before she could make much progress, the vehicle stopped and the rear door opened. Stewart pulled her roughly from the car onto hard, muddy ground.

'Out you get, my girl,' he said gaily. 'And don't bother trying anything as nobody can see us or hear us.'

It was hopeless to struggle. She felt revulsion as Stewart picked her up in a fireman's lift; he was stronger than he looked and only grunted slightly as he shut the car door. Clarice looked around but could see nothing but drifting fog and a high hedgerow. She must try to find out where they were, she realised.

It could not be the country, as they had not driven for long enough. There had been a steep hill and then a descent; she realised they must be somewhere on or near Hampstead Heath. Then there was the sound of metal rattling; a muffled curse and then a crunching noise, as if Stewart were breaking open a lock. Then there was the creaking of unoiled hinges, and they were suddenly inside a dark, musty smelling room.

Stewart flicked on a battery torch and Clarice could make out dirty whitewashed walls and a dust-laden floor, and then they were on a spiral staircase, going down and down, the air becoming warmer with each step, as if they were entering the very bowels of the earth.

Cliff stopped to gasp for breath; he was not used to running or physical exertion of any kind, and it took him several seconds to reach the side road into which he assumed Stewart's car must have turned. He peered through the fog at the street name: North End Terrace. It was a cul-de-sac, so where the devil had the car gone? Then he saw it, parked tight up against a hedge and almost obscured by foliage.

He looked around desperately; where on earth could they have gone? There were no houses at this end of the road, only a rough track which led past some back gardens, to some sort of brick-built shed or garage at the end. He looked down and saw heavy footprints on the muddied track, the heel-marks deeper than one would normally expect, as if a man had been walking with a heavy burden.

He considered for a moment whether to bang on the doors of one of the houses and demand that the police be telephoned, but he could not afford to waste any time. Stewart and Clarice must be in that shed, or garage, or whatever it was. Yes, the padlock hasp looked as if it had been forced apart. He crept to the door as quietly as he could, and flung it open.

Inside he could barely make anything out, but it was clearly empty. He felt a warm blast of air and a rumbling sound from the corner. Lighting a match, he saw a metal staircase spiralling downwards, with some sort of official notice above it bearing the name of the Charing Cross, Euston and Hampstead Railway.

Of course! This must be connected with the tube line, and the 'ghost station' that Clarice had enquired about. Far below, he could hear the sound of heavy footsteps on the metal stairs, and he followed as quietly as he could.

Eventually the staircase reached platform level and he peered through the gloom; there was just enough emergency lighting here to enable him to see his way without having to light a match, which would surely attract attention.

The shape and layout of the platform appeared similar to other stations on the line, but this one was coated with the dirt of ages, and heaps of equipment and supplies, many of them covered with tarpaulins, were stacked against the walls. He crept along the platform edge to keep out of sight, then heard a rumbling noise. There must be a train approaching, he thought, but before he could move, an explosion of light and sound took place as a train roared through the station at what seemed an impossible speed.

Cliff was thrown back, dazed by his head and shoulders coming into contact for the briefest of moments with some tiny portion of the train. He collapsed into a heap of tins and boxes, and felt warm liquid seeping down his back. My God, he thought, I'm bleeding.

An instant later the train had gone and the station was silent again; he winced with pain and then bit his lip as a metal lid of some sort rolled onto the track with a clatter.

Then everything went black.

'Who's there?' shouted Stewart. Clarice saw him walk cautiously along the platform, shining his battery torch ahead, and then heard him chuckle.

'Blasted junk all over the place. Nothing to worry about my dear,' he said, returning to Clarice. 'I'm getting jumpy. Just a bit of metal falling off the platform. You needn't worry, as nobody's going to disturb us. Nobody knows we're here.'

Clarice squirmed uncomfortably on the ground as she felt objects sticking into her. Stewart noticed her movements and smiled.

'You ought to be more comfortable for this,' he said. 'I'll get a tarpaulin.'

As he moved away from her, Clarice increased her efforts to release her bound wrists. She could feel jagged edges under her, cold, rusty metal. It must be some sort of discarded bracket, she decided, with screws sticking out. Frantically she worked one of the screws into the knot of cloth, and felt it give way sufficiently for her to almost free her wrists.

Then Stewart returned and tucked a heavy, foul-smelling tarpaulin under her head. He stepped back and looked down.

'My, but you are awfully pretty,' he said, as if he were admiring a dog or a horse. 'Better than that friend of yours, Evelyn. She was a painted harlot, that one. All show. I followed her most nights. I know what she was up to with that oily little friend of hers near Hendon. I had to teach her a lesson, on the tube of all places. And what luck the train stopped when it did! That Philpott woman, and Wilby's wife, they weren't much better either. And as for that stupid little Vera, what a disappointment *she t*urned out to be! But you, you're a natural beauty. Oh, I'm going to enjoy this!'

Clarice screamed from behind her gag. To her surprise, Stewart pulled it off and leant forward, his face inches from her own. She prayed that he would not detect the minute movements of her wrists as she finally worked her hands free behind her back.

'Scream as much as you want, dear,' he said. 'In fact, I find it rather adds to the enjoyment. I've always had to cut the fun short before, because I've never managed to get one of my lady-friends in a quiet spot like this.'

'You're wrong,' gasped Clarice, as confidently as she could. 'People *do* know about this place. Hitting that policeman was a mistake. It will bring them here. In fact I expect they are coming here right this minute. Your wife will tell them everything.'

'Nonsense, my dear,' said Stewart. 'She won't say a word if she know's what's good for her. And don't think your Mr Hargrove will help. Or should I say Colonel Wilby? Oh yes, I know who he is all right, but he's not as clever as he thinks. The great *pukka-sahib* confident he can outwit a lowly char-wallah like me. I've set him up for a fall though, you'll see. Or rather you *won't* see. By the time anybody works out where we are, I'll have…'

He howled in agony as Clarice brought the heavy iron bracket up from behind her back and slammed it into the side of his head.

He grabbed the improvised weapon and brandished it at her. 'You bloody little…' he began, and then stopped, whirling his head around.

'Who's there?' he shouted.

Light fell on his face, and Clarice gasped as she saw the deep bloodied cut she had inflicted on him. She looked to her right but could not make anything out, only the glare of a beam from a battery torch.

'Get away from her, Stewart,' said a loud voice, which she recognised as that of Inspector Travers. 'You haven't a chance, so I suggest you come quietly.'

'Where's all your friends, then?' taunted Stewart. 'I think you're on your own, Inspector. So I'll say cheerio. I'm taking the girl with me.'

Before Clarice could react, he seized her arms in a vice-like grip and pushed her ahead of him, pulling the gag upwards onto her throat and tightening it until she gasped for breath.

'Think what you like,' said Travers. 'But let the girl go. I've had the trains stopped on either side of this station, with my men on board. They're upstairs, too. There's nowhere to run to.'

Stewart laughed. 'You think I don't know other ways out of here?' he asked. 'This place has been my little personal dungeon for months. I know every nook and cranny. And I don't fancy your chances following me along those live electric rails.'

Clarice felt herself pushed roughly along the platform edge, but then confused sounds echoed all around her. She saw Travers run towards them and launch himself at Stewart, who struck out with the metal bracket. Travers dropped heavily to the ground, his hat rolling away across the platform.

Then there was the crash of heavy boots on metal, and more lights pierced the gloom as three policemen entered the platform from where Travers had been standing.

Stewart began running along the platform, dragging Clarice with him as she struggled desperately to free herself from his powerful grip.

Then a figure emerged from behind one of the large piles of equipment and dealt Stewart a heavy blow across the head with a lump of wood, as if he were a batsman hitting a six. Her heart leapt as she saw in the torch-beams of the policemen behind, that it was Cliff.

She ran into him, almost colliding with him and causing him to lose balance slightly.

'Run as fast as you can!' he shouted. She needed no further encouragement and clambered across the heaps of equipment to the other end of the platform. Then she stopped and turned to look as she heard Cliff call out again.

'Stewart, don't be a damned fool, you can't get away!'

'See if I don't,' yelled Stewart, and ran to the platform edge close to the black maw of the tunnel. In the torch light she saw something glisten under his feet, and he lost his footing, skidding around momentarily like an ice-skater badly executing a pirouette.

He overbalanced and fell heavily off the platform edge onto the live rail below. There was an enormous blue flash and a cloud of evil-smelling smoke, and then the sound of a man's feet banging dementedly on metal, as if demonic drummers were rapturously welcoming Alec Stewart into hell.

'It was oil – and there was me thinking it was blood!' joked Cliff. 'I must have spilt a tin of the stuff when I was knocked back by the train and passed out. So I really didn't do much at all. Stewart slipped on the oil and fell on the live rail, and well, that was that.'

Clarice and Cliff sat side by side on the sofa in the sitting room of the Lovell Villa Private Hotel, a few days after the fatal incident at Bull and Bush station. Colonel Wilby – formerly known as Mr Hargrove – stood by the fireplace puffing on his pipe. Mrs Sibley and Miss Grant had been summoned in addition by Inspector Travers who had arrived to update them on the progress of the case.

'I wouldn't say that, sir,' said Travers. 'If you hadn't hit him with that bit of wood and dazed him, he could have got away into the tunnels. It's like a maze down there and we hadn't had time to get the current turned off. I wouldn't have risked sending my men after him and I was in no condition to go down myself.'

He fingered the piece of sticking plaster on the side of his head that covered the wound inflicted by Stewart on the platform.

'And I'm glad to see you looking well, Miss Thompson,' he added. 'You put up a jolly good fight yourself.'

'I did what I could,' said Clarice. 'But if you and Cliff hadn't turned up, I doubt I would have been able to hold him off.'

'Oh, it doesn't bear thinking about,' said Mrs Sibley, feeling her neck. 'To think, I was harbouring a dangerous criminal under my roof all that time. And him with impeccable references.'

'You weren't to know, Mrs Sibley,' said Travers. 'He fooled his landlady at his previous address at North End Terrace, just as much as you. We think he was out pretty much every night, prowling the streets looking for women. And we also think now the old station entrance was where he took Miss Philpott.'

'Was that the young girl who got away?' enquired Miss Grant.

'That's right, madam,' said Travers. 'We think Stewart

found the disused entrance while he was out prowling one night, and realised it would be a handy place to finish off his next victim, who turned out to be June Philpott. Fortunately Miss Philpott managed to escape, but she wasn't lucid enough to identify the place.'

'And that's how Mr Stewart was able to disappear from the train after Evelyn was killed,' said Clarice.

'Correct,' said Travers. 'It was a stroke of luck for him that the train stopped when it did. Most people wouldn't have known about the ghost station, but Stewart knew there was an exit to the street level, and jumped at the chance. Otherwise he risked being caught when the train arrived at Hampstead.'

'You seem to know an awful lot about the movements of a dead man,' said Cliff. 'How on earth do you know so much?'

'We've got most of it from his wife,' said Travers. 'She was covering for him. She knew what he was up to because he told her about it, confident that she wouldn't do anything because she was scared of what he might do.'

'But why didn't she just leave him?' asked Clarice. 'Surely anything was better than staying with him?'

'It wasn't as simple as that,' said Travers. 'Stewart had a strong hold on her. Not only was she afraid of him physically, but he was all she had. She had no money of her own, no job, no family. Without him she couldn't act the Lady of the Manor, or whatever they call them out in India.'

'The Rajah and Rani,' said Cliff thoughtfully. 'I always thought she played that up rather a lot.'

'That's because she was trying to hide who she really was,' said Travers. 'Her maiden name was Mukerjee, and her mother was some sort of hostess in a disreputable hotel. Her father was a European, British perhaps but nobody's sure.'

Miss Grant inhaled sharply and Mrs Sibley simply exclaimed 'Well!'

'She's what they call a Eurasian out there,' continued Travers. 'Mixed Indian and European blood. The Indians don't like them much and nor do the British, eh, Colonel?'

Colonel Wilby puffed contentedly on his pipe. 'I'm sorry to say you're right, Inspector. Such people get a hard time purely through accident of birth. And in England they often don't fare much better, although they can cover their tracks more easily here. I can quite see why she didn't want her husband to expose her. That doesn't mean I think she should be let off, by the way.'

'She won't be, sir,' said Travers. 'The commissioner's pushing to have her charged with aiding and abetting, but at the very least she'll be convicted of obstructing the police in the course of their duty. She'll be away for a long stretch, whatever happens.'

'Forgive me, Mr Hargrove, oh dear, I mean, Colonel Wilby,' said Miss Grant. 'I still don't quite understand where you fit into things. Why go under an assumed identity? Colonel Wilby is such a nice respectable name, much preferable to plain old John Hargrove.'

Colonel Wilby smiled sadly, an expression that Clarice realised she had seen often on his face. 'As you know by now, my wife was murdered in Bombay. I was away on active service in Waziristan – the North West Frontier – at the time and I wasn't able to return until the trial was over.

'A friend of mine was the defending barrister for the young Indian boy, Ajay Dass, who was accused of my wife's murder. He wasn't happy about how the police conducted the investigation and had a theory that it was actually Alec Stewart who was the killer.'

'He admitted to me in the tube station that he killed her,'

said Clarice. 'But why wasn't he found out?'

'Stewart was cunning,' said Wilby. 'He knew how the justice system in India worked and he was able to exploit their prejudices. He'd met my wife at the Scots kirk – they were both Presbyterians, you see – and befriended her while I was away. I suppose she was lonely, with me being away so often. After he'd lured her to a park and...and killed her, he must have noticed there was a Congress rally going on nearby.'

'Congress?' asked Cliff. 'You mean the independence fellows?'

'That's right,' said Wilby. 'Nationalists. Not well liked by the authorities. Stewart said he'd come across my wife's body by chance and seen a group of boys running away shouting nationalist slogans. Feelings were running high in Bombay at the time and the authorities felt they had to make an example. Poor young Dass was in the wrong place at the wrong time. He was lucky to avoid hanging, although he's still rotting in prison for manslaughter.'

'And that's when you started to look into the case, sir?' asked Travers.

'That's right. I became convinced that there had been a miscarriage of justice, but if you know India, you'll know that was a powderkeg which could blow up in my face if I handled it wrongly. I had to get hard evidence that Stewart was my wife's killer. And so I started to have him investigated. I tried private enquiry agents but they were not much use, and I decided to get involved myself. I suppose then it became something of an obsession. When Stewart and his wife suddenly left India, I became even more suspicious.'

'Mrs Stewart said they left India for her health,' said Clarice.

'I knew that was poppycock,' replied Wilby. 'She didn't

have malaria or any of the illnesses for which the British get sent home. Stewart had a good position and had years to go before retirement, so why chuck it all in unless he was worried something was going to be found out? I was convinced he was going to get away with it and that's when I decided to chuck in the towel myself and follow them to England under an assumed name.'

'But why use a false name?' asked Mrs Sibley. 'I should have been perfectly happy to give house room to someone called Colonel Wilby.'

'Thank you, Mrs Sibley,' said Wilby, 'but I had to make sure Stewart didn't realise I was on his trail. I used the name of a friend in Ceylon, John Hargrove, who has business interests in London, which I could use as a cover if anybody started to look too closely into my true identity. Eh, Inspector?'

'It worked well, up to a point, sir, I'll give you that,' said Travers.

'Thank you,' continued Wilby. 'I took a room in the same street as the Stewarts – North End Terrace – and I kept a watch on his comings and goings.'

'Of course,' said Travers, snapping his fingers. 'That's why you had that attic room. Windows front *and* back.'

'Well spotted, Inspector,' said Wilby dryly. 'I was convinced if I could watch him for long enough, he'd give himself away. It was a sort of madness, I realise now, but when June Philpott was found half-strangled nearby on the Heath, I was sure that would lead to his arrest, but nothing happened, and then he aroused my suspicions further by moving away again.'

'That's when he came here,' said Clarice.

'That's right,' said Wilby. 'By this time I was nearly desperate and I decided not just to live in the same street, but the same house. I was pretty sure no photographs of me had appeared in the Indian newspapers, and since I had changed my name, I thought it was worth the risk that the Stewarts might identify me.'

'And did they?' asked Cliff.

'He told me he'd realised,' said Clarice.

'I'm pretty sure he *did* realise who I was,' said Wilby. 'But by that point I was past caring. I had begun to be a bit reckless, following Stewart around at night in the hope of catching him in the act. I even used the same trick to get back into the house that he did, by jemmying the window. I learnt that one from house-to-house searches in the army.'

'We're pretty sure he knew who you were, sir,' said Travers. 'We think that's why he stole your Indian Army tie from your room, and used it to strangle Evelyn Parks, then planted it back in your room later for us to find, and why he stole your other tie – the green and yellow one – and why he wrote John Hargrove on the label. He wanted you to be the chief suspect in the murder of Miss Parks *and* Miss Beech. And I'm sorry to say, it worked – for a while at least.'

'No harm done, Inspector,' said Wilby. 'I'm afraid it's me who should be apologising. Stewart carried out two murders and one attempted murder, and each time I, who was supposedly keeping watch on him, wasn't doing anything of the kind. To think, when that poor servant girl was killed, I was only a few feet away, and I didn't even notice.'

'I don't understand,' said Clarice. 'Where were you when Vera was killed? We assumed you had gone on the run.'

'I did, but not very far,' said Wilby. 'I'm used to camping rough on the North West Frontier with my men, keeping out of sight for weeks on end. It comes naturally to me. I spent some time on the Heath, then realised the best place for me was in the garage here, hidden under the tarpaulins at the back.'

'You mean you slept in that cold garage?' exclaimed Miss Grant. 'You poor, poor man!'

'Believe me, it was more comfortable than Hampstead Heath,' said Wilby with a smile. 'I know a few people in London and was able to get food and bedding and so on discreetly. I kept a regular watch on the house as best I could, but even I had to sleep sometimes, and that's when Vera was killed.'

'Yes,' said Travers. 'Miss Thompson's explanation for that makes sense now. We all assumed it was Colonel Wilby – or rather, John Hargrove – who had come back to the house and strangled Vera. But it was Stewart, who had merely gone downstairs, crept round to the side window and climbed in, then gone back into the house through the flowerbeds. That's why Miss Thompson didn't hear any footsteps on the gravel drive at the front.'

Travers turned to Wilby. 'I just wish you'd come to the police with all this first,' he said. 'It might have saved us all a lot of bother.'

'I couldn't risk it,' said Wilby. 'The police in India botched my wife's case, and the Hampstead police botched the June Philpott case too, as far as I could see. I couldn't risk it happening again. I was determined I was going to find some piece of evidence that would hang Stewart – or even catch him in the act myself. In the end I didn't even manage that. I couldn't even stop him kidnapping Miss Thompson here.'

'You mustn't blame yourself,' said Clarice firmly. 'You did everything you possibly could. Your wife would be proud of you.'

'I suppose so,' said Wilby sadly, looking down at his

pipe which had now gone out.

'What will you do now?' asked Cliff. 'After the inquest, I mean.'

'Go back to India,' said Wilby decisively. 'On the first passage I can get, to clear Ajay Dass' name. That will be quite an undertaking, but it's the least I can do. And it's what Jean would have wanted. You see, India's all I know, really. I've spent all my life there. A place like this – foggy old London – is as alien to me as the Hindu Kush is to you people. I miss the sun, and the snow-covered mountains on the Frontier. There's something...*clean* about it.'

'I'm sure there's no shortage of cleanliness in this house,' sniffed Mrs Sibley. 'I can't see that you've cause to complain about my standards of hygiene.'

'Of course not, Mrs Sibley,' said Cliff quickly. 'I believe Colonel Wilby was speaking metaphorically.'

'Thank you, Thorley,' said Wilby. 'I should love to stay here as long as I can, Mrs Sibley, until the inquest is over. I assume I can continue to remain as a paying guest until then?'

'Yes, of course,' said Mrs Sibley. 'But on that point, I'm sorry to say I have an announcement. Two residents of this house have been murdered, and that's more than a respectable person can bear. I've had a very generous offer from a builder – he's Irish but you can't have everything – who wishes to purchase the house and convert it into flats. That's the thing these days, he says, what with servants being so hard to find. So I regret to inform you all of two months' notice.'

Mrs Sibley folded her arms and looked defiantly at the assembled company.

'But what about Miss Grant?' said Clarice with concern. 'After all she's been here since 1899.'

'That's very thoughtful of you, my dear,' said Miss

Grant, 'but I shall be quite all right. I have a cousin in Bath who has invited me to reside with her. London is going down somewhat, these days, but Bath is still very respectable I am assured. I shall be moving to the Pulteney Private Hotel.'

Clarice smiled. Somehow it was inevitable that someone like Miss Grant should never be released from the potted ferns and stained glass windows of respectable private hotels.

'Well, I'll let you get on with discussing your private business,' said Travers, standing up. 'I'll be letting you know in due course about court appearances and so on.'

'I'll show you to the door,' said Mrs Sibley, but Clarice stood up quickly.

'It's all right, I'll go,' she said brightly, assuming correctly that the landlady did not like taking on such trivial duties in the absence of servants.

At the front door there was a moment of silence as she and the Inspector looked at each other.

'I...'

'I...oh I'm sorry, Miss Thompson. You go first.'

'I just wanted to say thank you properly. For what you did. I'm lucky to be alive.'

'I made a hash of things,' said Travers. 'Let that brute knock me out cold. It's Thorley you need to thank.'

'Yes I know, but if you hadn't got there as well with your men it might have turned out differently.'

Clarice noticed the man was blushing, and quickly changed the subject. 'They won't be too hard on Mrs Stewart, will they?'

'It's not for me to say.'

'It's just that...I only had to put up with him for a few minutes. It was beastly but it didn't last long. I can't imagine what sort of torture he must have put his wife through over the years. She must have been terrified.'

'I'll do what I can for her,' said Travers. 'You can speak for her at the trial, I imagine.'

'Yes I hope so. Well, goodbye Inspector. And thank you.'

'Goodbye, Miss Thompson. And thank *you*.'

'Not interrupting anything, am I?' said Cliff as Clarice closed the door. 'Bit of a shock about the hovel closing down, eh?'

'I can quite understand it,' said Clarice. 'Poor Mrs Sibley will struggle to get residents when they find out what went on here. Perhaps it's for the best.'

'Where will you go?'

'I've rather had it with Hampstead after all that's happened,' said Clarice. 'I shall be qualifying at the college soon, fingers crossed, and getting a bit more money coming in, so I can afford somewhere a bit closer into town. What about you?'

Cliff beamed with pleasure. 'I've just sold another article on the case – to one of the Sundays – and they've offered me a permanent position. That means I'll be able to afford something better as well. Where will you be moving to?'

'I thought of West Kensington.'

'What an extraordinary coincidence. That's exactly where I've been planning to move to.'

'Since when?' asked Clarice, a look of happy suspicion spreading over her face.'

Cliff laughed. 'Since you just told me!'

THE END.

Other books by Hugh Morrison

A Third Class Murder
An antiques dealer is murdered in a third class train compartment on a remote Suffolk branch line. The Reverend Lucian Shaw, travelling on the same train, believes the police have arrested the wrong man, and begins an enquiry of his own.

The King is Dead
An exiled Balkan king is shot dead in his secluded mansion following a meeting with the local vicar, Reverend Shaw. Shaw believes that the culprit is closer than the police think, and before long is on the trail of a desperate killer who will stop at nothing.

The Wooden Witness
After finding the battered corpse of a medium on a remote Suffolk beach, Reverend Shaw is thrust into a dark and deadly mystery involving ancient texts and modern technology.

Death on the Night Train
Reverend Shaw is called to the deathbed of an elderly relative in Scotland by an anonymous telegram. Soon he becomes embroiled in a fiendish conspiracy which reaches to the highest levels of the British establishment.

Murder in Act Three
When a cast member is killed during an amateur dramatics performance in the village hall, everyone thinks it was just a terrible accident. Everyone, that is, except Reverend Shaw. But can he find out the truth before the killer strikes again?

Murder at Evensong
The unpopular Dean of Midchester dies in a fall, and Reverend Shaw suspects foul play was involved - but can he prove it?

www.hughmorrisonbooks.com
Order from Amazon or your local bookshop.

Printed in Great Britain
by Amazon